Women Lie Men Lie 2

Lock Down Publications and Ca$h

Presents

Women Lie Men Lie 2

A Novel by **A. Roy Milligan**

Lock Down Publications
Po Box 944
Stockbridge, Ga 30281

Visit our website @
www.lockdownpublications.com

Copyright 2020 by A. Roy Milligan
Women Lie Men Lie 2

First Edition 2020
Printed in the United States of America

Lock Down Publications
Like our page on Facebook: Lock Down Publications @
www.facebook.com/lockdownpublications.ldp

Stay Connected with Us!

Text **LOCKDOWN** to 22828 to stay up-to-date with new releases, sneak peaks, contests and more...

Thank you.

Submission Guideline.

Submit the first three chapters of your completed manuscript to ldpsubmissions@gmail.com, subject line: Your book's title. The manuscript must be in a .doc file and sent as an attachment. Document should be in Times New Roman, double spaced and in size 12 font. Also, provide your synopsis and full contact information. If sending multiple submissions, they must each be in a separate email.

Have a story but no way to send it electronically? You can still submit to LDP/Ca$h Presents. Send in the first three chapters, written or typed, of your completed manuscript to:

LDP: Submissions Dept
Po Box 944
Stockbridge, Ga 30281

DO NOT send original manuscript. Must be a duplicate.

Provide your synopsis and a cover letter containing your full contact information.

Thanks for considering LDP and Ca$h Presents.

CHAPTER 1

Kelly sped off as Marvin followed behind her. While driving she began looking around the car for any of JC's personal belongings. She opened the glove compartment first, nearly swerving into the next lane. Marvin blew the horn as soon as he noticed, which caused Kelly to regain focus. Her hands were shaking and her mind was racing. She heard her phone ringing seconds after that.

"Yes Marvin?"

"What the hell are you doing?!"

"What, what you mean?"

"You swerving all over the damn road!" He yelled.

The last thing he wanted was her to get pulled over by the police and get caught with the gun she had on her. He wanted so badly to tell her to pull over so he could secure the gun from her, but he didn't bother, he just wanted to get out of the area as quickly as possible.

"Calm down, I was not swerving all over the road Marvin. I was trying to see if he left something in here so I can throw it away."

"Throw it away where? Just wait until you get to the dealership to do all of that! You can look around in the car when you get there, but for right now, stop doing all that extra shit!"

Kelly was quiet for a few seconds before she said, "Whatever Marvin." Then she went back silent, still holding the phone and waiting for the light to turn green. She was doing her best to sound normal when she talked. Although her voice was a little cracked from the tears she was holding back. All she could think about was what she had just done. Kelly wished she hadn't done it and began reminiscing about the times she had with JC. His face kept playing over and over in her mind and she knew if Marvin found out she had sex with him, he would kill her.

CHAPTER 2

"Kelly, you straight? Why you quiet? Tell me how things went, did you take care of everything in there?" Marvin asked.

"Yeah, that was simple. Most of them were already sleep," she said, trying to code herself and not be so descriptive over the phone. People had been catching cases left and right talking on the phone like no one was listening and Kelly wasn't trying to become a victim.

"You sure they was all sleep?"

"Yeah Marvin, of course!"

"What's your problem? Why you getting loud with me like that?"

"I'm not. You keep asking all these questions like I don't know what I'm doing or something. Then we're on the phone. Why can't you just wait until we stop to talk?" she asked.

"Damn, I was just asking. Calm down."

"I'm going to the car lot, I'll see you there." She hung up and drove through the yellow light, leaving Marvin stuck at the red light. She turned up the radio and continued to think about JC the whole way there.

"Bitch!" Marvin said, as he heard her hang up in his face. He was so mad, he wanted to choke her. She was acting weird and he didn't know why.

Kelly had no problem returning the car to the dealership, but the problem began when she got into the Hummer with Marvin. He was already mad at her for having an attitude with him for unknown reasons and when she hung up on him it just pissed him off even more. "You lucky these kids with us because I don't appreciate the way you acting right now. You on some straight bullshit right now."

"How Marvin?"

"What's wrong with you?" he asked, driving off almost ramming into another vehicle until the driver blew his horn alerting Marvin he almost hit him. Marvin just ignored him and kept driving and tending to Kelly.

CHAPTER 3

"Pay attention before you kill us all!"

"Tell me what's wrong with you."

"Hi Mommy!" the girls yelled, after saying it three times before, but getting ignored.

Kelly turned around, looking into the backseat to see them both sitting right next to each other smiling. Kelly smiled thinking about how much she loved and missed them. "Hi beautiful girls!" Kelly said, reaching for the both of them. She got up and nearly climbed all the way in the back just to hug and kiss them.

"Mommy, I'm hungry."

"Me too," the other one said.

"We'll get something in a second. Sit back," Kelly demanded.

"I asked you to tell me what's wrong Kelly," Marvin said.

"Nothing's   wrong.   I'm   fine."

"Well, why you acting all bitchy?"

"You act like I'm supposed to be happy and jolly or something. For God's sake, I just shot and killed two people. How do you want me to act? I'm still shaking and nervous as hell, hoping no one seen or heard anything."

"We straight, you don't have to worry about that. Just make sure you get rid of that gun tonight."

"I know."

Marvin smiled as he looked at Kelly. He was proud of her and he was happy that their plan worked so well. "Okay, I'll leave you alone."

"Thank you."

"You're welcome, give me a kiss," he said as he leaned over and puckered up his lips and started moving them like a fish. Kelly giggled and leaned in meeting him halfway for the kiss as he was driving.

CHAPTER 4

After Marvin got the kids some tacos to eat, he drove straight home to count all the money he just gained. Kelly wasn't happy and he seen it in her face while he was counting the money on their California king size bed. It was just him and Kelly inside their room while the kids were in the next room playing. Marvin could feel the tension in the air and he still couldn't pin point what the problem was. He had done several jobs like this with Kelly and he knew she was solid and had no problem shooting or killing for him, but for some reason this time was different. He had never known her to react how she was.

"Don't forget to set aside the $10,000 we owe Welma," Kelly reminded him as she watched him making separate piles of money.

"I got her right over there. But this big pile right here is for Merido, $60,000 cash," he said, proudly smiling and looking at all the hundred dollar bills. "You want to take this over to him?"

"Not really. I just want to relax right now. I don't feel too good," she said, hoping he would just leave her alone.

"So you want me to take them both their money?" He asked, licking his finger before he separated more bills.

"That would be nice."

"Okay. I'll take care of that, since you did the hard part this time, I'll drop the money," he offered.

"Did you call her yet?"

"Who, Welma? Yeah I called her, why what's up?" He asked.

"I was just asking because when I called she didn't answer and that was right when we walked in the house."

"Oh, she was probably just getting off from work. I talked to her though and she sent me a time to meet her through text message so that's taken care of. I'll hit Merido off first then I'll go to Welma."

"Well, I'll give the kids a good bath and make sure I catch the news," Kelly said, as she kicked off her high heels.

"I'll be back shortly," Marvin said, as he loaded all of Merido's money into a brown paper bag and put Welma's inside his pocket.

"Bye, be careful. I love you," Kelly said.

"I love you too," he replied.

Marvin left out the door jumping into Kelly's Escalade and driving to a store Merido had that was about thirty minutes away. Marvin rode with the music loud and all he could think about was Kelly. He wondered why she was acting so weird as if she wasn't happy about all the money. He remembered the day Merido told them about JC and how much money would potentially be involved. Kelly's eyes had lit up when she heard the amount and now it was like she didn't even want the money nor did she care about it. Many thoughts passed through his head all the way until he arrived and walked through Merido's door where he was ringing up one of his customers.

"And that comes to… $7.84," Merido told his customer. The old white lady gave him a ten dollar bill. He gave her change back and she walked out the door with a smile.

"Marvin, what's up buddy?" Merido shouted with a big smile on his face. He could hardly wait to hear the breaking news.

CHAPTER 5

Marvin smiled as he shook his hand across the counter. "What's up? The job is done and came out very nice. Next time give me something a little easier than that. He was crazy as hell man! He was killing up some shit. If I was the Feds I would have locked him up forever."

They both laughed.

"You got a point there."

"I didn't know he was that crazy though. I knew he was wild but not that wild," Merido explained.

A customer walked in and interrupted, "Can you tell me how to get to the Yak from here?" A tall light skinned woman asked. She was wearing a pink dress with matching heels. She looked like she was on her way to a party. Marvin was checking her out and wanted to say more to her, but he stood there and kept quiet.

"The 'Yak'? What's that?" Merido asked, looking at Marvin.

"Pontiac. They call Pontiac 'Yak town'," Marvin said smiling.

The girl rolled her eyes at Merido and turned to Marvin. She stood there with her hand on her hips, "Can you tell me where to go?"

"Yeah, just jump on Telegraph and take it until you see a road called Franklin, make a right and go straight into the Yak."

"Okay. Thank you. So which way do I go, north or south?"

"North."

"Thank you," she said, heading for the door.

Marvin shook his head admiring her big booty, "You're welcome."

"Fuck that bitch, I didn't know what the hell no 'Yak' was," Merido said with an attitude.

"Chill out man, it ain't that serious."

"She was disrespectful though bro."

"You know how chicks be, fuck it. Back to this nigga JC. He was nuts!"

"Did you take care of everything?"

"Of course, here you go," Marvin said as he pitched the bag of money to Merido balled up with a tight knot. Merido caught it and noticed that it had some weight to it. He opened it and smiled as soon as he seen all the green bills sitting on top of each other. None of it looked like it came from the bank, it looked as if it came from the streets by how rough the bills were. Marvin had everything rubber banded up for him.

"How much?"

"That's all of it. $60,000 to yourself, enjoy."

Merido smiled hard and came around the corner to hug and kiss Marvin on the cheek. "Man, I love you!"

Marvin laughed at how happy he was to get the money. "I love you too. Thank you."

"No problem," Merido said grabbing him and kissing the side of his head. He was so excited, he didn't know what to do with himself. It was all over his face and he could not stop smiling.

"Well I know things have to be hot right now so make sure you take which ever car you were into Bobby so he can get rid of it for you."

"We didn't use a car. We caught him in a house."

"You had to drive there right?"

"Yeah."

"Get rid of the car."

"Damn, are you serious?"

"Yeah! I'm serious. You really think it's safe to drive a fucking getaway car around?" Merido pointed out.

"It wasn't done like that though. It-."

"I don't want to hear it Marvin, get rid of it. Call Bobby as soon as you leave here. I'm serious. And after that, take a trip. You hit big. Go treat yourself. Have some fun."

CHAPTER 6

Marvin really didn't feel that getting rid of his Hummer was necessary, but he was going to do it just to be safe. "A trip sounds like a great idea. I think Kelly would like that also. Fuck it. That's what I'm going to do. I'mma take me a trip. To where? Not sure yet. I'll run it by Kelly and see what she says."

"Well go ahead and get out of here. Have fun and make sure you bring me back a souvenir from wherever you guys decide to go."

Marvin chuckled, "I won't forget about you." He said as he was going inside his pocket to answer his phone. It was Welma.

"Hello."

"Are you around?" she asked.

"Yes and I need to see you, like right now."

"I'll be home in about two minutes, I just turned on my street. How long will it take you to get to my condo?"

"I'll be there soon," he said smiling and hanging up. He knew Welma wanted him to meet her at her house for a reason.

"She got you blushing, whoever that was," Merido said as he watched Marvin's cheeks turn red.

"No one important. This money got me blushing, not her. I'm out, I'll talk to you soon," Marvin said, walking in an aisle and picking up a box of condoms and sticking them inside his pocket. He threw up the peace sign and rushed right out the store. Merido just shook his head and smiled.

When he arrived, he drove into Welma's garage and parked. She had to have heard him drive up because as soon as he turned the vehicle off, the garage door began to go down slowly making it dark until Welma opened the door. Marvin walked inside.

"Hey!" she said smiling and giving him a big hug. She was wearing a see through purple robe with matching three piece lingerie set underneath.

"Damn you look good and you smell edible. You looking real fine right now baby. Is all this for me?" he asked as he checked her out.

She gave him a quick grin, "No, I'm waiting for someone special," she said becoming irritated with his voice. She thought he was a sweet young man and very handsome, but sometimes he would over do things and she didn't like it. His voice drove her crazy. He sounded like a broke down Keith Sweat.

CHAPTER 7

Marvin looked at the serious expression on her face, he was waiting for her to say she was playing or at least smile, but she wasn't budging. "Oh well, maybe next time then," he said, walking past her and slapping her on her booty.

She laughed, "No, this time. I was just playing with you. This is all for you," she said.

She caught up with him and turned him around and began kissing him softly with wet kisses all over his neck.

Welma laughed, "I'm not going to give you a hickey. I know you have your little girlfriend to go home to," she said, then continued kissing on him.

Marvin lifted her up and carried her to the bedroom while tongue kissing her the whole way. He was already excited from all the extra money he had just finished counting. He couldn't wait to get inside of her. When he laid her on the bed, he began taking off his shirt, pants, and shoes.

Welma was lying back while he crawled on the bed and dug his face right between her quivering thighs. He licked all around her pussy until it was drenched with his saliva. Welma was breathing hard and he hadn't even started yet. He kissed around her pussy and between her soft thighs before he went to licking all over her clit. He licked and licked while working two fingers inside her pussy.

Her eyes were closed and her mouth was wide open, but she couldn't say a word, all she could do was put her hands over her face. Soon, she came hard, making a huge puddle in the center of the bed.

Marvin continued to lick and suck for a few more minutes then he made his way up to her perky titties.

His tongue danced around her nipples and soon he grabbed his throbbing dick and eased it inside of her pussy. She was soaking wet and he only lasted a few minutes before he pulled out and nutted all over her pussy lips. He collapsed right on top of her and Welma just shook her head in shame. She laid there and thought about how JC used to put it down. There was no comparing the two of them. JC was only one of three people in her life that knew how to put the dick down on her the way she liked it. She loved the way Marvin ate her pussy but she hated his sex.

CHAPTER 8

Welma patted Marvin on the back and told him to get up. She walked to the bathroom and he followed her. As she sat on the toilet and peed, he turned on the shower and got in to clean himself up.

After he was done, he gave Welma her money for letting him put cameras in her home so he could watch JC.

"So is JC dead?" she asked.

Marvin smiled while grabbing his keys from her dresser. "Just watch the news tonight and you tell me."

Welma shook her head already knowing what he meant. "Well thank you for saving my life." She then gave him a hug and a kiss on the cheek. He had tricked her into thinking he was a private investigator.

He had showed her paperwork and everything else. After seeing that, Welma knew he was certified, or so she thought.

"No problem. Thank you."

"You're welcome."

"Take care, I'll talk to you soon."

Marvin left out, heading back home. He checked his phone and Kelly had called seven times. He knew he was going to get cussed out. As he dialed Kelly back, he thought about the money Welma had in the bank. She was also on his list. She had to die as well.

"What's up baby?" he said, as soon as he heard Kelly pick up the phone.

"Don't, what's up baby me. Why didn't you answer the damn phone? Do you know how many times I called you? Merido told me you had been left from up there. I called Welma and she didn't answer either, now all of a sudden both of ya'll calling me back at the same time. Imagine that."

"Kelly chill out, I left my phone in the truck. You always trippin' for no reason. It ain't my fault the old bitch had to count her money five times without thinking I was ripping her off."

"Whatever. She's old?"

"I mean yeah, she looks older than she really is."

"Oh," Kelly said. She wanted to ask more questions about Welma, but she didn't want to sound too insecure.

"She's an older lady, nothing to trip over. I don't want nobody but you," Marvin explained.

"I'll see you when you get here. If you hurry up, you can catch the news and see for yourself that the job is done," Kelly told him.

Marvin laughed, "I didn't doubt you, and I know you put it down, but I'll be there shortly. Did you want anything while I was out?"

"No I'm good. See you when you get here, bye."

"Love you, bye" he said, but Kelly had already hung the phone up. She still wasn't as happy as he expected her to be and it as kind of bugging him.

By the time Marvin arrived, Kelly was still sitting on the couch watching the news, but it had just jumped to a new subject.

"Did I miss it?"

"Yup, it just went off too. They say one victim survived."

"What? I asked you if you made sure they were all dead, what the fuck?! What if that nigga still alive?"

CHAPTER 9

"Calm down, it's a girl that's alive," she didn't wanna hear his mouth anymore.

"What else they say?"

"Not much. The Feds was investigating trying to link some other murder up with that one."

Marvin didn't say anything and just watched the news until it went off. He was hoping that it said something more about what happened, but it didn't. "So now we need to find out who the girl is. What if she seen you Kelly? I told you all head shots nothing less. What the hell?"

"I did!" she said, getting up and rushing to the bathroom. She shut the door and all she could think about was JC. She knew she had to keep Marvin away from the T.V. until she figured something out or else he would find out that she didn't shoot JC in the head. Seconds later she heard him by the door.

"You lucky it was a girl. Because I was about to say."

She opened the door with an attitude. "You was about to say what? I've always handled my business Marvin and you know it. I took care of what I was supposed to take care of!"

"Okay cool, don't worry about it then. I thought you was about to say JC wasn't dead."

"Yeah whatever, let me smell your dick," Kelly said walking up to him and unzipping his pants and pulling them down. Before she smelled him, she looked up at him and he had the most confident look on his face and he wasn't resisting at all. He stood there and let her sniff him out, knowing that he was clean and had nothing to worry about. She grinned once she was done smelling his dick.

"What?"

"Nothing, just making sure you're not sticking your dick in someone else's pussy."

"You only accusing me because you feeling guilty about fucking that nigga JC."

"Whatever Marvin, I told you I didn't have sex with him, I didn't have to. He was eating out the palm of my hand from day one."

"So you telling me, you begged me to stay all those nights with him, claiming that will be the only way we will be able to get him, and he never tried to eat your pussy or fuck you? Bullshit!"

"I told you he tried to have sex with me and eat my pussy, but I rejected him and he respected that," she said as her face begin to turn red at the thought of when she had sex with JC popped in her head.

"Put it on our kids that you didn't have sex with that nigga or suck his dick."

"All I did was kiss him and I told you that. Why don't you believe me? Did you have sex with Welma?"

"No I didn't and never will. I'm not attracted to old wrinkled ass women."

CHAPTER 10

"Oh now she old and wrinkled, just the other day you was just-"

"Don't try to reverse shit on me! I said put it on our kids that you didn't have sex with JC!"

"You put it on our kids that you didn't have sex with Welma!" she fired back.

"I put it on my kids that I didn't have sex with that old bitch," he said with an attitude.

"And I put it on our kids that I didn't have sex with JC or give him head. You happy now? Dick head," she said, as she walked away from him and went into the bedroom and slammed the door. She opened it and said, "Oh, you can start packing your shit too! Your dick smells like Zest soap. All we use here is Dial asshole!"

Marvin's stomach dropped to his drawers, "Get the fuck out of here with that. Dial is not the only kind of soap I use!"

Kelly came out the room, "Ok, well show me in this house where some damn Zest is!"

Marvin stood there speechless. There was nothing he could do. There sure wasn't any Zest soap in the house.

---

10 days later, Diamond was waking up out of the coma from a gunshot wound to the head. Cradle had been up there with her for a week now, but today there was him and five of her other family members as well. Diamond blinked her eyes twice before she fully opened them.

"Hey lil' soldier," Cradle said.

Diamond just smiled and looked around the room. She had no idea where she was until she saw the flat screen hanging on the wall, rotating ceiling fan and the foot of the hospital bed she was in. That's when she remembered what happened to her.

CHAPTER 11

"You sleep good?" he asked.

"Is she woke?" her little cousin asked.

"Her eyes opened, wandering all around the place. She smiled at me too," Cradle said, happy to see that Diamond was being strong. He wanted her out and well, but he knew it would take a minute for her to get 100%. He was just tired of being up at the hospital all day wondering if she was going to make it or not.

Diamond blinked her eyes a few times and turned her head towards the other family members that were inside the room. She then smiled at them and said "Hi," in a soft low voice bringing tears to everyone's eyes. They were all shocked she had made it through and was now trying to speak.

As Diamond lied in the hospital bed getting better, the police had been back and forth up there questioning her for about two weeks now. They showed up around the same time each day and they were doing everything they could to get Diamond to give them information.

"Where is JC?" the detective asked but got no answer. She took a deep breath and struggled to talk. "What else do you remember about him?" the detective asked. Diamond just turned her head and looked at Cradle before she began to talk.

"He came in and there was a bunch of fighting going on in the other room," she said, as she paused for a minute and began to cry. "I couldn't see what was going on because I was in the other room tied to the bed with my friend," she said. Her voice was deep and raspy.

"What happened when JC finally came in the room you were in?"

"He was shot, all bloody. And the tables had somehow turned, and Chip was holding the gun to him.

They talked for a moment and a white girl came in and shot them both."

CHAPTER 12

"A white girl?" the detective asked, as he started writing it inside his note pad. "Then what?"

"I dozed off and I woke up in this hospital."

"She's lying! You don't believe that crap?!" the other detective asked.

"Why? You don't?"

"Hell no! It's clear this was all over a drug deal gone bad, she's trying to save her own ass. There's more to the story than that. Tell us the truth!"

"Aye both of ya'll need to go. She's done talking," Cradle said, as he stood up and began leading them to the door.

They followed him, but they were both mad. "She's going down if she's lying. Don't think for one second that we won't find out what went down."

Cradle didn't say anything, he just closed the door behind them and walked back to where Diamond was lying in the bed crying. "I told you don't talk to them motha fuckas. All they gonna try to do is act like they know what happened, try to get you to twist your words and story up then do they best to try and charge you with whatever they can. Don't you think if they had some solid shit you would already be charged? If they had solid shit, they wouldn't have to ask you shit. These motha fuckas have been up here about six times in the last two weeks and they still asking the same shit. You never, and I mean never, talk to the police about nothing," he explained.

Diamond listened and cried nonstop. She wished she would have listened to her cousin the first time when he told her to keep her mouth shut. "Why he keep asking me questions about that boy?"

"Because they've looked at the phone records of you talking to JC and they think you know more than you telling them. They fishing, trying to see what they can get. As long as you keep your mouth shut, you don't have to worry about nothing. You don't have to talk to them no matter what they say. They will play their little games and try to trick you into talking by telling you that you are going to jail if you don't talk or they going to take your kids if you had any if you don't talk, but don't fall for that. Keep your mouth shut at all times."

"I know, I know Cradle. I'mma just tell them me and JC was just fucking that's all."

"You don't have to tell them shit. Fuck them! Let them wonder whatever they wonder. They don't know shit, they just think they do and thinking is not enough to charge a person with shit, so fuck them. Keep your mouth shut."

"Oh, ok. I won't talk to them anymore."

"Good," he said relieved.

Cradle was irritated with his cousin but he was glad she was coming back to her senses. He was just worried that she might slip and say something to the detectives. It was clear to him that she could easily be tricked into telling on herself or on someone else.

CHAPTER 13

As days passed by, Diamond was getting stronger. But all she could think about was JC because she had set him up to get killed. Today she talked to Cradle about the whole situation. He had been up there for three hours now and he was ready to go home. He told her to let him figure something out, but don't stress because everything was going to be taken care of ASAP.

Since Diamond was scheduled to be released in the morning Cradle left at nine that night. "I'll see you in the morning. I'll be here to get you first thing," he told her.

"You not going to stay up here one more night with me so you don't have to do all that driving?"

Cradle laughed, "Look at you trying so hard to keep me up here. I been up here every night with you since you been here, let me get a little break."

"Oh my God, whatever, Cradle. Go then. Bye," she said with

attitude. She ignored him as she used her remote control to change the channel on the T.V.

"You mad at me?"

Diamond was silent. She didn't even look his way.

"I love you," he said waiting on a reply.

"Whatever Cradle. I love you too."

Later that night Diamond tossed and turned in her hospital bed for nearly two hours. All she could think about was JC. It felt like he was in the room with her and that scared her. She was about to call someone just to talk to until she fell asleep, but instead she just grabbed the newspaper article off her table. It was the article relating to her being in the hospital. She read it five times and wished she could change what it said.

CHAPTER 14

Around one in the morning, Diamond finally dozed off into a deep sleep and around 2:30 a.m. she awakened to someone patting her on the shoulder.

"J-," she was cut off by a rough choke hold and several punches to the face that felt like a hammer was hitting her each time. There was no scream from her, just a painful death that lasted not even three seconds.

The next morning Cradle was on his way to pick her up until he got a call, "I'm on my way cuz," he said as soon as he picked the phone up. He knew it was Diamond, she had been calling from the same number on the caller ID since she had been in the hospital.

"I'm sorry. Hello," an unfamiliar voice said.

"Who dis?" he said shouting over the loud music that played in the background.

"May I speak to Creg please?"

"Yes, speaking, sorry about that. I thought you were someone else," he said, turning the music down a little.

"It's okay. Can you please turn your music down a little more for me?"

"Yeah," he said turning it off. "Ok."

"I have some really bad news for you. This is very unexpected," the nurse on the other line said.

Cradle thought nothing of it. "Ok?" he said, thinking she was about to say Diamond will have to stay a little longer. "What is it?"

"Demika Lineheart was killed last night in the hospital bed."

Cradle couldn't believe what he was hearing. He was speechless.

"She was brutally beaten and choked to death. The police have no suspects as of right now," she said, but Cradle had dropped the phone.

"Sir….Sir, sir."

Cradle began punching is steering wheel. "Fuck! Fuck! Fuck!"

Although the lady said they had no clue or leads to who this could have been, Cradle didn't care, he had his own leads.

CHAPTER 15

Around 3:35 a.m. Merido was sitting behind the counter inside his store when a customer walked in to buy some cigarettes. It shocked him when his next visitor walked in. He thought he was looking at a ghost but this was not ghost. Merido thought about reaching for the 357 mag he kept behind his counter, but he didn't. He tried to just play everything cool and calm.

"Hold on a second," he said, as he exchanged money with his customer. "$3.12 is your change. Thank you and have a good night."

"Thank you," the guy said before he took his cigarettes off the counter and walked out the store.

"What's up? You look like shit. What happened?" Merido asked, staring JC right in his eyes. He could see that JC was dealing with a lot. He looked rough in the face, like he hadn't slept in days.

"A bunch of shit is going on right now. A bunch of shit that don't make sense right now."

"Well I don't know exactly what's going on, but if I can help you let me know. You know I got you on whatever you need lil bro."

Merido wasn't sure if he knew about him or not. "I thought you was in a shooting or something. There was some guys in here the other day and your name came up. One said you were shot. The other one said you were dead. What is going on?" Merido said, moving closer to where his gun was.

"Yeah I got shot, but it's going to take more than that to keep a nigga like me down," JC said as he stood there in some filthy blue jeans, a dirty white tee shirt that was ripped on the side, some muddy boots and a brown hat. Merido had never seen him like this before. "I need a favor. I have some serious business to take care of. I ain't got no money, clothes, food, or a car right now, but I got a whole lot of money put up. I have to go get it though and I promise I'll give it back to you."

"No problem man, you know I got your back, hold on a second, "Merido told him while walking to the back not taking his eyes off JC. He had a shot gun that leaned against the wall. He knew if he didn't finish JC off in the store it would be a big problem. He knew JC was very dangerous and right now he was full of rage. He looked as if he didn't care about anything.

CHAPTER 16

Merido didn't want JC to find out about him and come for him later, so it was time to put a bigger hole in JC. He went over to the camera system and cut it off. He could easily kill JC and say he was trying to rob the place.

Merido picked the gun up knowing it was already cocked and loaded. He peeked at JC and he was just standing there looking out the door not even paying attention to where Merido had gone.

Merido aimed and had a clear shot of JC's chest. He went to squeeze the trigger and in came another customer which made Merido drop the gun and rush out there. He greeted the customer and then went into his wallet to give JC a wad of money.

"Here, this is $1500. But hold on a minute, I want to talk to you some more after this customer leaves, plus I have some more money in this cash register that I can give you."

"Thanks, but this is more than enough. I really appreciate this, but I have to go. The police is looking for me and who knows who else is looking for me. Shit is crazy right now and I don't want to put you in danger due to my actions."

"No, no wait a second. Tell me what happened so I can know what's going on. I'm scared for you right now," Merido said, trying not to talk too loud. "Let me get you some protection or something."

"Naw man, I'm good. Help your customer. I'll be back soon, I gotta go," JC said, moving towards the door.

"Just wait three seconds, I'll be right back, "Merido said going to the back. He was going to kill JC and the other guy that was in there shopping. He would just put a gun in both of their hands and say they were both trying to rob the store. Merido grabbed the gun and by the time he came back to the front, JC was gone. "Fuck!" he said, running to the phone to call Kelly.

"Hello," she said with a sleepy voice.

"Kelly! JC is alive and he just left my store!" Merido shouted.

The guy that was shopping made his way to the cash register with some chips, pop and candy and looked like he was ready to pay. He waved to get Merido's attention and Merido looked right at him and told him he could have it.

"I know. I was going to tell you," she said getting out of the bed that she shared with Marvin.

She hadn't told Marvin yet either because she didn't want him to be mad at her.

"What?! Oh shit!" he said, as his eyes grew wide when he realized there was a gun in his face.

"What?" Kelly asked.

Merido was quiet as the guy that he thought was a customer was really a robber. "Open the cash register now!"

"Ok. Just calm down. Take the money," he said, as he opened the drawer and gave the guy all the money inside.

The guy ran out the door and Merido finally took a breath and went back to the phone where Kelly was still saying 'Hello'.

"Yeah," he said.

"What are you doing?"

CHAPTER 17

"Nothing. I just got robbed."

"Oh my God! Are you ok?"

"Yeah Kelly, he just wanted money. I gave it to him and he took off running. When were you going to tell me about JC? Why didn't Marvin tell me!?"

"Stop yelling and let me explain. He doesn't know either, so keep this between me and you please."

"I don't know what you have going on, but you better fix this shit. We are dealing with a fucking lunatic!" he said, making his way to the door to lock it. He had enough for the night and he was ready to call someone in to work for the rest of the night.

"Trust me, I can handle this. I'm going to take care of everything. You have nothing to worry about, JC doesn't know you have anything to do with what is going on. So just playthings cool until I come back from this vacation. I'll finish the job myself."

"That's what you said before. You were supposed to finish this Kelly! What the hell were you thinking?

This guy will kill us all!"

"I will, I promise. I'm sorry."

"How long before you get back? You need to tell Marvin right now and ya'll need to come back now before things get out of hand, I'm telling you Kelly. He looked like he was ready to kill everyone. I don't trust this fucker."

"Two weeks and we'll be back. Marvin can't know. JC won't do shit, he's wanted right now. He will lay low for a minute," she said.

"You better hope you're right Kelly," he said, before hanging up on her.

JC had nowhere to go. He didn't know who to trust. Trusting Kelly almost cost him his life. It was dark out on the streets and most of the cars on the road were police, so JC walked through the alleys, jumping fences and going through backyards.

He was heading to Welma's house and although he caught her cheating he had to go somewhere to relax until the morning so he could get his thoughts together. There was no way he was going to a hotel around here, his face was all over the place on posters and flyers that read WANTED.

CHAPTER 18

It took him a while to get to Welma's condo, but he finally made it. He knew she seen his face all over the news, but he was also confident that he could explain to her what happened.

He crept in through a window that was always kept unlocked. It was so dark when he stepped in. He was hoping that she was there because he didn't see any cars in the driveway, but he figured she had them both in the garage. He was also hoping that she didn't have company over.

He tip-toed through her place until he reached a bathroom. The whole place smelled like chicken and he was hoping she had some left because he was starving.

Luckily he knew his way around because there weren't any lights on until he cut the bathroom light on.

He walked closer to Welma's door and saw that it was slightly cracked. He pushed it open just enough to where he could slide through and walked closer to the bed where she was snoring softly. He was happy there was no one else in the bed with her or things would have gotten out of hand.

He wanted to wake her but didn't want to scare her. He felt like a stalker but he needed to rest and Welma's is where he went. He backed away from her bed slowly not wanting to make too much noise and finally he flicked the light on to see if she'd wake up. She didn't move, so he flicked it off then on again and Welma's eyes opened and focused right on JC's.

She jumped as soon as she recognized him and dove for her phone that sat on her nightstand by her bed, screaming "Help! He's going to kill me!"

JC wasted no time. He ran and dove right on top of her to stop her from dialing on the phone. "Chill out, no one is going to kill you, especially not me," he told her, as he grabbed her and wrapped her up so that she couldn't move. He then took his loose arm while lying on top of her, and hung the phone back up.

"Let me go!" she screamed.

"Shut the fuck up Welma, before someone hears you. I'm not here to kill you ok," he said, putting his hand over her mouth.

"Why the hell would I kill you, stupid? What the hell are you talking about?"

She tried to talk but he still had his hand over her mouth. All she was able to do was hum and slob over his hand.

"I'mma let you talk, but don't scream or call the police. You know me way better than that. You know I'd never hurt you," he told her as he slowly moved his hand from her mouth.

She jumped up to her feet standing in front of him, "What is going on? Your face is all over the news JC. A private investigator supposedly killed you because you were killing people and was out to kill me.

CHAPTER 19

"What is this shit JC because nothing is making sense to me right now?"

"What?" he asked, looking confused. "What private investigator?"

"A guy said he killed you to protect me."

"What? Who?"

"Marvin, the guy who drove the Hummer truck. You said you knew him."

"Marvin?" he said, thinking to himself. He couldn't figure out why he would lie to Welma. "What do you know about him?"

"Nothing. How did you get shot or did you? Why is everyone lying to me?" she shouted, grabbing her head.

"Calm down, I'm not lying to you. You can trust me," he said, walking up to her and holding her. "I promise you can trust me. I did get shot, but I'm still living. I was set up."

"What do you mean you were set up? Set up for what? What did you do so badly? It doesn't make sense to me." She cried on his shoulder hoping she really could trust JC. "Why would they want to kill you?"

"They after money. It's a long story, but please just trust and believe that I'mma handling this. The guy Marvin is a phony, stay away from him. When was the last time you seen him?"

"Recently, he dropped this money off," she said running to her closet and grabbing the box she had put the money inside of.

"He gave me ten thousand dollars."

"For what?" he asked confused.

"To put cameras inside my house," she explained.

"What? What are you talking about? Tell me the truth Welma, the whole story not half of it!"

CHAPTER 20

"Ok, he gave me ten thousand for letting him spy on you. He put cameras around the house to spy on you."

All JC could think about was the night he was lying in the bed with Kelly and she told him that she had a private investigator spying on him.

"Why would you do that? Where is the camera Welma?" he asked becoming mad.

"They're gone, they're gone now," she said. "He told me you were a murderer and that you were going to kill me for the money I had in the bank. He knew how much I had in my account and everything."

It was clear to JC that Marvin had lied to Welma just to get to JC and it was clear that Kelly and Marvin were working together. "This shit is crazy," he said as he was putting the pieces together in his head. He sat up on the bed wondering how they knew about him from the beginning, but that wasn't as clear yet.

"What?" Welma asked, as she stared at him rubbing the top of his head.

"This bitch."

"What bitch?"

"This white bitch tricked me. I can't believe I let her trick me like that. That bitch got me good too."

"Well you not the only one that got fooled. Marvin fooled me too."

"Are you sure that you don't know anything else about him?"

"Just that he's a private investigator. He showed me the paperwork and everything. He even had a badge."

"What was the name on the badge?"

"I don't remember."

"Damn Welma, you was supposed to pay attention. You just let this nigga tell you whatever and you fell for the shit."

She shook her head, "I'm sorry. I am so sorry JC, I swear."

"Don't worry about it. I'mma find out what the fuck is going on."

"Let's just call the police and let them take care of it," she said.

CHAPTER 21

He looked at her like she was crazy. "Are you fucking crazy? That can't happen. It's a lot of other shit going on that you don't know about. Just let me handle this my way and all this shit will be over. Right now, I really need you to just help me out and trust me, please."

Welma looked him directly in his eyes and seen that he was serious. She didn't know exactly what was going on but she was willing to trust and help JC. His mind was all over the place. Kelly was the number one topic.

JC couldn't even sit in one spot, he must have sat down and stood up four times since he arrived. He also was thinking about what he would say to his mother. How will he confront her? All these things ran through his mind and it was almost overwhelming.

"So can I stay here until I get myself together?"

"Yes JC, of course," she said, walking over and hugging him. She couldn't help but to cry because she felt sorry for him. "I miss you so much JC, I am so sorry for everything that happened. I will never do anything like that again. I'm so sorry."

"It's ok…we both did wrong... I was fucking up too. I'm sorry too."

Minutes later, they pulled apart from each other. "You stink. You need to get your stinky butt out of them clothes and take a long hot shower."

He laughed for the first time in days. "I know," he said pulling off his shirt and making his way to the shower. He was filthy. "Fix me some of that chicken you got down there too. I smelled that shit outside!" he shouted from the bathroom.

Welma laughed, "Yes sir!"

JC had bathed himself four times and dirt was still rinsing off of him. As he continued to bathe himself, he glanced at all the wounds he had on him. He shook his head and turned the water off to get out. He was still iffy about trusting Welma and he decided to watch her closely.

CHAPTER 22

B eing wanted by the police was a lot scarier than he had imagined. There was nothing fun about it and it made it hard to trust anyone. He was always looking over his shoulder making sure no one was looking at him funny. With his picture all over the T.V., it was easy to be spotted in a store or anywhere in public. He didn't want to become the person that goes into a store then as he is leaving out, there are five police cars waiting on him because someone inside noticed him and called the police to turn him in for the reward.

JC wrapped a big gray towel around himself and he vowed that before he died or went to jail that he would kill Kelly, no matter what.

When he walked out, Welma had his food ready. JC ate like he hadn't ate before and he was still hungry, but he didn't ask for more. Welma watched him the whole time and when he was done she took his plate to the kitchen.

"I feel a lot better now," he said.

"You thirsty? I got some pop down there and some of your favorite Kool-Aid."

He smiled, "Bring me some Kool-Aid please."

Welma came right back and handed him a glass of cherry Kool-Aid. "Where are you sleeping? With me or in the guest room?"

He laughed as he sat on the bed wrapped in a towel. His muscles were glistening from the water that was dripping down his body. You could see the cuts in his arm, and his six pack.

There ain't no way I'm going to sleep far away from this bitch after what the last bitch just pulled, he thought to himself.

"When have I ever slept in the guest room?"

"I was just asking. I didn't know if you wanted to be alone or not." She explained climbing on the bed and getting underneath the covers. "I worked 15 hours straight today, I'm exhausted. Goodnight," she said.

"Goodnight," he replied.

CHAPTER 23

J C tried sleeping but there was so much on his mind it was hard. Welma was on the other side of the bed snoring again. JC just laid there staring at the ceiling before finally going to sleep.

Around 8:00 a.m, Welma woke up in the bed by herself. She looked around the room and didn't see or hear JC anywhere in. She then looked at her dresser to see if he might have left in her car, but her keys were still there. She got up and found him sitting at the computer. "I should've known."

"Sleep good?" he asked.

"Yeah, actually I did. You want me to go out and get you some clothes?"

"Yeah that would be nice. How about you just run up the street and grab me some tees and sweatpants and I'll order some real clothes online."

"Ok. Whatever you want. Hope you don't get tired of me. I

don't go back to work for a month. So I'm all yours if you want me."

He smiled, "Really? The whole month?"

"Yup."

"Why so long?"

"They're doing construction in the area I work in. I could have worked downstairs, but I was given the option to take it off with pay, so of course I took that."

"Yeah I woulda too. Well everything should work itself right out because I don't plan to go anywhere anytime soon, police been all over the place."

Welma was quiet for a second then she finally said something. "The murders they're trying to charge you with, did you really do them? I'm just curious, I'm not-."

"No. I didn't do it," he said, cutting her off.

CHAPTER 24

"Well, why don't you just turn yourself in and I'll personally help you get a good lawyer."

"I can't right now. I have some people to see first."

Welma shook her head in disbelief. "Oh, so that's what's going on?"

"Until I can take care of some things, I can't turn myself in just yet."

JC directed his attention back to the computer and he began searching for a store to shop at. "Thanks, I really appreciate this too," he told her.

"Don't worry about it. I made $10,000 off your ass," she said, joking.

He laughed. "I might have to use the car in a couple days, if that's okay with you."

"JC you alright with me. No problem, anything you need just ask me."

JC stayed on the computer for hours. He even built up the courage to call his mom, but it went to voicemail right away. The phone didn't even ring. He tried to reach her on social media, as well but her page no longer existed. He knew that she had to have seen the news and realized that she had slept with her son. He wanted to go on his own page, but he didn't want to be traced so he left it alone.

Welma was the only person that knew his whereabouts and he wanted to keep it that way as long as he possibly could. Things had to cool down.

Cradle drove to his friend Angel's house. He knew she could help him out with some things. He had just hung up the phone with her, letting her know he was on his way and now he was knocking at her door.

"What Cradle? What brings you by, I haven't seen you in months," he smiled at her, but she could tell something was bothering him.

"I need you to help me with something."

CHAPTER 25

"Ok, no problem. You ok?"

"Not really. I lost my cousin Diamond recently," he said.

"Diamond? Aww man, what happened? That used to be my girl."

"She as involved in some bullshit, fucking with this nigga they call JC. That's why I'm here. I need you to find some family members of his for me."

"Cradle, don't. Let God deal with him. I don't want to see you get in trouble, I already know what's on your mind.

"Naw, you don't have to worry about me, I ain't gonna do nothing. That's what I got goons on my team for."

"Ok, what's his name? If it wasn't for Diamond, this would've cost you."

"What would it cost me Angel? I'm sure I could afford it."

"See, I don't want your money. You know what I'm talking about."

"That's what you got a man for. Why you still trying to play?"

"Ugh! See, I knew you was gonna be talking that bullshit. He is horrible in bed and you know that. I need some good dick right now and you gonna give it to me right after I look up this info for you."

"Naw Angel, I'm not in the mood for this, I'm trying to take care of business."

"I know, I know you upset, but just let me make you feel better. I promise you'll like it."

"I always do, but not today Angel, shit is--."

"Pleeeaasse! Just this one time. I know I'm not going to see you for who knows how long, just let me fuck you and suck your dick this one time."

Cradle said nothing. All he did was sit on the couch and watched her while she worked with the computer and pulled up JC's family members.

"Ok, his mom's name is Vanessa Fisher and she lives in Romulus."

"Does it have an address?"

"Yup, I'll write it down for you. You want aunts and uncles too?"

"Yeah, please," he said cheering up and taking off his jacket. Angel's house was nice and bright. She had yellow and white everywhere. The computer was even yellow. The living room had yellow leather couches and white tables. Cradle had never seen that before.

"Where you get these couches from? I know you had to get them imported or something. I ain't never seen no shit like this. How much these couches hit you for?"

"A pretty penny nosy, and yes I got them imported from Italy.

"So where is yo man, he not coming anytime soon is he? I don't want to have to fuck that nigga over."

She laughed, "Shut up! He's out right now. He should be home in a few hours or so."

CHAPTER 26

"You betta find out when he coming. If he come up in here talking sideways, I'mma beat his ass. You already know how I get down, so call him," he insisted.

"Ok, damn Cradle. Crazy ass always wanna fight somebody."

He laughed. "You heard what I said, call that nigga, for I fuck his ass up."

"I heard you for the 5th time. Let me write this information down for you. So that I can call him so he won't come and beat you up," she joked, but Cradle took her ass serious.

"Shiit, not me. Matter of fact, come here. Fuck that whack ass nigga. Here, come suck this dick," he said pulling his dick out. She turned around and seen his pants to his ankles.

"Boy you is a mess!" she said giggling, walking over to him and getting on her knees. She first folded the paper and put it in his pocket then she put his dick in her mouth and started caressing his balls. Cradle threw his head back and just enjoyed the pleasure. He had been so stressed out and Angel took his mind somewhere else within seconds. He looked down at her and she was slurping and stroking his dick like she hadn't had any dick in months. She had his dick sticking straight up while deep throating him. "You ready for this pussy?" she asked.

"Yeah let me see how that pussy feel, it's been a minute."

"Oh you forgot?" she asked while taking off her yellow stretch pants. "You got a condom?"

CHAPTER 27

"You know it," he said, pulling out a gold wrapper that was empty. "Damn, hold on, I know I got one," he said, looking through his pants but finding nothing.

"You don't have any back there?" he asked, referring to her room.

"No, me and my man don't use condoms."

"Well I don't have none. You still want to do it?"

"Yeah of course, I'm on birth control anyway."

"Birth control ain't gone protect you from HIV."

"Cradle stop ruining the moment. My pussy so wet, feel it." Cradle stuck his hand right between her legs and it felt like she had just came on herself. She was slippery and very moist.

"Fuck it," he said as he positioned her to straddle him on the couch. She set on his dick and her moans were unstoppable. She was shouting while bouncing up and down on his dick.

Cradle cupped both butt cheeks and bounced her even harder on his dick. "Ahhh! Fuck me, Fuck me!" she begged as she slobbed all over his ear and neck. Her eyes were rolling into the back of her head, and she was having the time of her life. Cradle continued to stroke her deeply and she took every inch of him at a speed that was so fast, her whole body locked up. Cradle was getting ready to cum so he began bouncing her roughly up and down. Her pussy was wet and soft inside and Cradle was loving it. It was so good, but before he came, he stopped and switched positions.

"Let me hit that pussy from the back," he said, pushing her off him.

"Noo, it's gonna hurt," she whined, turning over slowly.

CHAPTER 28

"No it's not, turn over," he said, flipping her over and pushing her back down. He shoved his dick back inside her wet pussy while she lied flat on the couch. He had one leg off the couch and one leg on and he was riding her ass. He began pounding her pussy so hard, her pussy was talking back to him for 10 minutes straight. Angel had her face in a pillow and was moaning non-stop until she heard the locks on the door. Cradle hopped up and grabbed his pants off the floor. All he saw was a short dark guy standing there with a surprised look on his face.

"What the fuck is going on?" he asked, looking at the both of them.

"Jerry, I can explain!" Angel said as she ran over to him with only a t shirt on. Cum was running down the back of her legs.

"Explain what? Who the fuck is this?" Jerry shouted as he smacked Angel to the floor. By this time, Cradle was fully dressed and mad at himself that he left his gun in the car.

"Chill out man, don't touch her no more," Cradle said, trying to stay calm because he didn't know whether or not this dude had a knife or a gun on him.

"This my girl, I touch her whenever, however-----." Cradle was on him before he could finish his sentence. Cradle began beating him in the face with his fist until Angel pulled him off screaming, "Stop! You're going to kill him!" But Cradle was still hitting him and finally snapped out of it when he saw all the blood leaking from Jerry's face, Jerry didn't even have a chance.

CHAPTER 29

"I'm outta here, I told you to call this bitch ass nigga before he popped up. This nigga fucked up my nut. I didn't even get my full nut off. I should finish fucking you right in front of this nigga."

"No Cradle, please go. I'm sorry Cradle, go!" she cried out while attending to Jerry.

Cradle left out with blood splattered all over his white casual snakeskin shoes. He got in his corvette and sped off.

"Bitch get the fuck off me," Jerry said, yanking away from Angel.

JC looked up Kelly's Escort Company. He Googled the name and all the information he needed was right there in front of him, including phone numbers and addresses. He wrote them down and he planned to visit them pretty soon, hoping to catch Kelly inside one of the houses. He could hardly wait to get ahold of her. He was going to make sure she had a very painful death.

"What do you want for breakfast?" Welma asked.

"Mmm, cook some of them good grits you be making," he said smiling. "And some eggs, bacon and biscuits."

"You trying to eat huh?"

"Hell yeah. I'm starving."

"Ok, you got it," she said, walking straight into the kitchen.

JC sat there clicking on clothes to order, still thinking about his mom. Every time he thought about what they did he wanted to puke. "Damn," he said, shaking his head trying to erase the image inside of his head.

Welma got up and began dialing the number again, but she still got no answer.

"He's not answering JC."

"Ok, fuck it. He'll call back sooner or later."

"It's clear you don't want to have sex with me but can---."

"Welma, honestly, you have no clue what I'm going through right now. My world is upside down. I don't even want to think about having sex. So please stop asking and trying. If you need me to leave for another nigga to come through and fuck you, I will and I'll come back when he's done. But with me, is out the question. My mind is somewhere else right now, I'm sorry."

CHAPTER 30

W elma was just listening. She could not believe the words coming from his mouth. She knew whatever he's dealing with had really taken a toll on him.

"Well I can respect that and I'm sorry," she said.

JC stood up and walked out of the room with her cell phone, calling Kelly's company.

"Hi, this is Rich, what can I do for you?"

"How long do you guys stay open?"

"24 hours sir."

"Ok, thank you," JC said hanging up. After breakfast, he got dressed and left, telling Welma he was taking the car and he would see her later. She paid him no attention and went back to sleep.

JC drove all the way to Pontiac and parked down the street from the house Kelly owned. He was hoping to see her.

Although she said she made her rounds in the morning, she could have been lying about that also. He sat out there for hours watching cars come and go. He saw plenty of girls in and out of there and finally decided to call and order a girl. He had stopped and bought a prepaid phone just for this particular experiment.

"Hi, this is Rich, can I help you?"

"Yes, I was calling to get a girl. I live right down the street."

"Ok, we can drop the girl off to you or you can pick her up. If we drop her off, it will be an extra $50, but since you live on the same street, it'll be $25."

"Well the problem is that I want a girl that has a hotel room. I have a wife and kids at home."

"Oh ok, sorry about that. Yes we have plenty of women that are set up in hotels," Rich told him. Rich gave him a few different phone numbers and told him to call them and set up an appointment. JC did just that and he was on his way to them right after he stopped by an old friend's house to buy two guns with silencers and no serial numbers.

He arrived at one of the best hotels in Auburn Hills and saw it was packed with cars and buses. He walked in and went straight to the room he was instructed to go to. He knocked twice before he got an answer from a beautiful Latina woman.

"Hi there," she said, opening the door for him to come in.

CHAPTER 31

"**D**amn baby, you fine as hell. You the one I'm fucking?" he asked.

She giggled, "Yes, I guess. There's nobody else in here with me."

JC was eyeing her from head to toe. She had wide hips and a small waist. She wore a pair of black booty shorts with a matching top that was cut at the belly, revealing her four packs. JC had come with the intention of murdering her, but he was thinking about having sex with her first. He walked in and she got down to business as soon as the door shut.

"So what brings you here?" she asked sitting close to him on the king size bed.

JC wanted to answer but he was too busy checking out the suite. Everything was glass and wood. It looked like a small apartment equipped with a separate kitchen and living room.

"Sir?" she said.

"Yeah, what's up?"

"What brings you here today?"

"Oh, I'm sorry. I'm just trying to live out my fantasy tonight."

"Well, what's your fantasy?"

"To fuck a Latina in her asshole."

She smiled. "I think I might like that papi."

"Well let's do it. How much is it?"

"$300 for anal sex."

"Damn, you an expensive hoe. Why you charge so damn much?"

"It's not expensive."

"Ok. Here," he said pulling his money out, counting out $300 and setting it on the table. "What you want me to do?"

"Get undressed and I'll do the same," she told him.

CHAPTER 32

J C could not keep his eyes off her ass. He loved the way she was shaped. She was just what he liked. And her facial features were even better. She was downright beautiful. Although JC came over to do some dirty work, he had stripped down to boxers within seconds. "Your turn," he said.

After she seen JC in his boxer shorts, she began to do a sexy dance for him while taking off all her clothes. She walked over to a small bag that sat in the corner on the floor to grab a condom and some lubricant gel. She squirted a small amount on her hand then pulled JC's boxer shorts down, rubbing the gel all over his dick, while watching it expand to its maximum potential. Looking at his size, she wasn't sure if she could take all of that so she walked back to the bag and brought the whole bottle of lubricant back and sat it on the right side of the bed. She then crawled onto the bed and JC followed while holding his stiff dick in his hand. She positioned herself doggy style, then arched her back, sticking her pussy out so much that JC stared at it. He wanted to make her scream. He put his condom on excited at the thought of fucking and killing her.

While he was moving closer, she spread her cheeks as far apart as she could. JC jammed his dick in, no sympathy for her.

"Ooohhh, Papi! Slowly!" she shouted, but JC was ramming as hard as he could. She did her best to run away from him but he tackled her from the back landing right on top of her with his dick still inside her.

He began to slow his stroke down as he felt her asshole getting wetter and wetter. She then calmed her moans of pain down as they turned into moans of pleasure. JC had his whole dick inside her and she was loving it. They fucked for about 15 minutes, until finally, JC nutted. He got up and took his condom off and started to get dressed.

"Well thank you," she said with a smile, feeling she got the better deal.

CHAPTER 33

"No problem," he said pulling up his pants. He waited until she turned around before he pulled his gun out. "Hey, you know what."

As soon as she turned around he shot her in the forehead dropping her to her knees then she fell on her face. He snatched his money off the table and began searching around the room wearing leather gloves. He had no luck finding any money until he looked under the mattress and found several hundred and fifty dollar bills. He stuffed them in his pocket and was headed for the door when he heard a knock. That didn't stop him, so he opened the door. "What's up?" he asked a man who looked like security.

"Hi, I'm here to see Liquid," the man said.

"Oh, come on in," JC said, letting him walk in to see her lying on the floor.

He quickly turned around trying to say something but JC let off two more shots to his chest. He walked out calmly, like a normal citizen leaving out of the closest exit.

As soon as he got outside, he called one of the other numbers he had got from Rich. "Hello." A sexy voice answered.

"What room are you in? I got your number from Rich and I have $500 for you. I'm outside right now."

"Oh, well, tonight is your lucky night. Come up to 345, third floor."

"Ok I'm on my way," he said, hanging up then calling two more of the numbers to get their room numbers as well.

He walked back in, first going to 345. He knocked twice and she opened the door and let him inside.

"Hi, you must be the one that just called," she said.

"Yup," he said as he walked in. As soon as she turned her back to him, he shot her three times in the back. There was no need for him to stay any longer, so he walked out of there immediately and went down the hall to room 367. He knocked once and the door opened up, there was a white guy walking out but he didn't give JC any eye contact. Then there was a short dark skinned girl waiting for JC to come inside. He did without saying a word and when she took her eyes off of him he shot her in the back four times and once in the back of her head. She didn't even get a chance to scream. JC closed the door and went to the next floor to room 444. He was about to knock until he heard a loud scream saying. "Call the police!"

He rushed to the nearest exit, running and jumping down flights of stairs headed straight to the car.

Before he started the car up and tried to drive off, two cars blocked him in.

JC quickly aimed his gun and started shooting at them both, hitting one officer in the neck and the other in the shoulder. He backed the car all the way out and drove out the parking lot but seen four more police cars coming his way. The cops called for backup and were right on JC's tail as soon as he turned on Opdyke Street.

CHAPTER 34

J C mashed his feet to the pedal driving 100 M.P.H trying to find the nearest highway. He blew through every light nearly wrecking at two of them. The police called for more cars because they were slowly losing JC due to the accidents at the intersection they were forced to stop at. Finally JC found I-75. He took that south and did 140 until he couldn't see the police lights anymore. He made it to Welma's house safe and sound, parking the car in the garage. If he would've been thinking, he would've realized that they had the license plate number and were now on their way to Welma's house while he was relaxing still sitting in the garage. As soon as he stepped out the car, he heard the police coming down the street full speed.

"Shit," he shouted, running to the door. He ran straight past Welma to the back of the condo.

"What's going on JC?" she shouted, but it was too late. JC had jumped through her glass window. Welma didn't know what to do. She just started screaming, especially when she heard the police kicking her door down.

"On the floor bitch!" one of the officers yelled as he pointed his gun directly at her head.

"Please stop, I don't—."

"Shut up! Where is he?" an officer demanded.

"I don't know! I don't know!"

The police searched through the whole condo, including the car they seen him driving and they couldn't find anything. JC was long gone by the time they realized he had jumped through the window, it was too late. Although they searched the entire neighborhood, they didn't find anything. "Who was just driving your car ma'am?" one of the detectives asked, wearing a cream suit and playing the nice guy.

CHAPTER 35

"I don't know sir, I'm sorry!" Welma said.

"Do you know that I can charge you with the four murders that were just committed?" he asked, looking her in the face, "One of our officers was killed."

Welma wasn't buying it. "You can try to do whatever you want, but I don't know what you're talking about," she said adamantly.

"Cuff her and take her down to the police station." Welma was cuffed and taken down to the police station.

After she saw the news the next morning, sitting in her cell waiting to get bailed out, she realized JC was crazy and wasn't a joke. She had no idea what had gotten into him. They showed the chase and the clipping regarding him being wanted for the other murders. The police still didn't know that they were chasing JC last night, but Welma was thinking about telling them. She knew he was in so much trouble and would rather see him locked up than dead. "Can I talk to someone?" she yelled through the bars. One guard walked up. "I want to talk to a detective about last night."

"Ok, let me call and see if he's available. Sit tight."

"Thank you." About a half hour later, Welma was being called out of her cell to be questioned. She walked inside a room where there was a table with about 15 chairs, but there was only her and two other men.

"Have a seat please," Detective Stewart said. Welma sat in the first chair she saw and they followed, sitting right by her. "So what do you want to tell us?"

CHAPTER 36

"I want to tell you who was driving my car last night," she said.

"Ok, that will help us out a lot," he said.

"It was Jason Cakes."

Detective Stewart's eyebrows raised at the familiar name, "Jason Cakes that's already wanted for murder?"

Welma began to cry and put her head down. She couldn't believe she had told them his name. She couldn't speak anymore all she could do was shake her head up and down to their questions.

"Are you scared of this man?" he asked.

She shook her head no.

"Are you related to this guy?"

She shook her head no again with tears falling from her eyes by the pound.

"Were you sleeping with him?" she waited a minute before nodding her head up and down.

"So you love this guy? Or should I say have some kind of love for him?"

She nodded her head up and down once again.

"Well just know that you are helping Jason out a lot because there are people after him that plan to kill him on sight, but if we get him first, he'll live, we want him alive," the detective said.

He realized that Welma couldn't control herself from crying, but he knew she'd be willing to talk more, just not right now. "Well Welma, we are going to let you go back to your cell and we'll come back to talk to you later before we release you." They walked her back to her cell and she sat there crying even more.

"My boyfriend is wanted for murder," she told the other girls in the cell.

CHAPTER 37

"Who is he?"

"Jason Cakes. Ya'll around his age, but ya'll probably know him as JC."

"Of course I know JC, he been all over the news," the girl said.

"How do you know JC?" Welma asked.

"Oh it was never anything between us. I know he used to be with my cousin Diamond, she got killed. People saying JC killed her too."

"Well I don't know what's going on right now," Welma said. That's when everything went silent and the girls started whispering to one another.

Welma had no idea they were planning on jumping her because they felt she knew something about Diamond's murder. Welma stood up and called for the guard after she seen how the girls were staring her down and sizing her up, especially Brittany, the one that said she was Diamond's cousin. The guard came just in time and Welma was out of there walking back down to talk to the detective.

"You bet not come back, you old bitch!" one girl yelled.

"That's why my cousin was fucking your boyfriend, you snitch ass bitch!" Brittany yelled.

"If I see you again I'mma fuck you up bitch!" the other girl shouted. Welma was so happy to get out of there, she was about to tell the detective everything she knew. She didn't know jail was so intense.

Brittany was walking back and forth in the holding cell. "I hope they bring that bitch back, I'mma fuck her ass up if they do," she said, walking over to where Welma was sitting to find some legal papers that had her home address on it. Brittany picked up the phone to call Cradle and gave him the address. He told her he would take care of it. He was so happy that he also told her he'd pay for her bail.

CHAPTER 38

L ater that night, Vanessa had just gotten off of work. She was so upset with herself after seeing JC's picture on the news. When they said his name, she almost passed out. She had no clue that he was her son before she made the mistake of having sex with him. She felt so stupid for losing contact for so long, to where she couldn't even recognize a loved one if she saw them, until it was too late. She had been crying all day. Her boss tried to send her home, but she didn't want to go home. She had no clue how she was going to face her son and explain to him how she had no idea what he looked like. She wondered if he even knew or not.

Vanessa got out of her car and walked up to her house unlocking the door and going inside. It was dark until she hit the light and was surprise to see Cradle sitting on the couch with two guns.

"Who are you?" she asked scared to death.

"Ask your son," he said raising both guns and letting off ten shots, six of them hit her and killing her instantly. Cradle left, leaving the door wide open so the murder would be discovered immediately.

He didn't care if JC ended up in jail before he could get to him, he was going to have him killed one way or another. Cradle called the guys he had watching Welma's house.

"What's up?" Zip answered.

"What's going on? Is that hoe home yet?"

"Yeah! She's been home, but the police are watching her house too, so we can't make a move yet."

"How many police cars are there?" Cradle asked.

"Just one, he keeps circling around the complex."

"Man, kill that mutha fucka! What the fuck you think, that's what I'm paying you for! I need this shit done tonight!" Cradle shouted.

CHAPTER 39

"Alright it's done man. You got it boss, I just didn't think you wanted—."

"Take care of that and bring that bitch to me," Cradle ordered as he hung the phone up.

Zip took his phone away from his ear. "He pissed off."

"For what, this shit hot. JC wanted all over this bitch, I ain't about to go to jail for nobody," Slaps said with an attitude.

"This is the plan, when the officer pulls over, I'mma creep up on him and pop his ass and you just run inside, bring that hoe out, and throw her in the trunk."

"That gun shit too loud," Slaps said, shaking his head. "Not down with this shit."

"We getting $30,000, it's whatever. Cradle wants the job done now. If you ain't with it, I'll do it myself."

Slaps shook his head. "Fuck it lets go."

They both waited until the officer parked and everything went as planned. Zip shot the officer in the head and Slaps knocked Welma out with his gun and drug her out the house, throwing her into the trunk.

Brittany had been out of jail for two days now, and she was back selling her crack on the block to pay Cradle back. Although she worked for Cradle, he was not going to bond her out at first. He was mad at her for not saving money for bond and a lawyer, but she learned her lesson. This time she planned on saving, and not just blowing her money on clothes and shoes.

Tonight the block was doing numbers. There were crack heads everywhere you looked. Brittany was walking down the street when she passed someone she thought was a crack head.

CHAPTER 40

"You straight?" she asked, as she stopped in her tracks trying to make another sale.

"Naw baby, you got the wrong one."

"Oh, my bad," she said, as she turned around and kept walking. Brittany was only seventeen and thought she knew everything. But knew nothing, especially when it came to boys she liked. She was only about 110 pounds soaking wet, but she had a very pretty face. She was light skinned with clear skin and could easily be mistaken for being mixed with black and white.

"Hey, come here real quick."

She turned back around. "For what?" she asked.

"Because I want your number," he said.

"You want my number? Nigga you ain't even got a car."

"Who ain't got a car?" he asked as if he had one.

"I'm just calling it how I see it," she said, walking back towards him. "Take that hoody off, let me see what you look like!" He did and she instantly knew who he was.

"Your name JC ain't it?"

"Yeah I use to fuck with your cousin."

"I heard you killed my cousin, that's the word and if you did I'm about to do your ass right here," she said pulling out her 380 glock and pointing it at him.

"Naw, Hell naw. Chill, I can explain. I didn't do that shit I swear, but I know who did. I swear I didn't do it. That was my baby," he pleaded mad at himself for letting her get the drop on him.

"So why my cousin after you?" she asked.

"Nobody believes me, but they will."

"What you mean they will?"

CHAPTER 41

"I'mma prove my innocence and if you don't mind, I could use your help." Brittany somewhat believed him and wanted to be on his side. She had known JC forever and she always had a crush on him, but she was always too young for him.

"How can I help you?" Brittany asked.

"Just fuck with me until this shit over with."

"What you mean 'fuck with you'?"

"Stay with me until I can get everything together."

"Nigga you on the run, you ain't about to get me killed."

"Naw I got a plan, if you trust me. Put that gun down though, people looking at your crazy ass, you drawing too much attention."

She put her gun up realizing, he had a point. "Ok, so what you about to do? Because you hot as hell in the hood. You need to get out of here."

"Well can you help me? I'll pay you whatever you want, I swear I got money. I got plenty of money, but you have to trust me, ok?"

"Ok JC, but if you do anything funny, I'mma do your ass in," she threatened him.

"Deal, you got a car?" he asked.

"No, but I can get one, that's nothing," she told him.

"Who car is it? It gotta be legit."

"It's legit, don't worry nigga."

"Can you get a rental car?"

"I can get anything you want."

"Ok well get us a room for the night because it's getting late and I ain't got nowhere to go. Everybody think a nigga on some bullshit out here, but they got the wrong nigga."

Brittany was beginning to feel sorry for him and wanted to help him. "Yeah I can get you a room, but I gotta grind out here," she said.

"Naw, I told you I need you to stay with me until shit is over. Whatever happens to me, everything goes to you. I got over a hundred thousand out here in these streets. Just trust me, I'mma take care of you as long as you look out for me. I need you to come to the room with me and stay."

"Hundred thousand?" she asked, thinking he was trying to play her.

"Over a hundred thousand," he corrected.

"And if you go to jail, it all goes to me?" she asked, clarifying.

"Why wouldn't it? You gone be with me right?"

"Ok," she agreed, calling one of her people to get a room. They went to one of the worst hotels in the city of Detroit, but JC felt extra safe because he knew there was no chance of any police coming where they were.

"Brittany, thank you so much. I have to tell you that I really appreciate the fact that you trust me right now. Please believe me, I'mma look out for you in a major way when I get everything straight.

CHAPTER 42

"That's cool, I got love for you, and you know that. I'm was just mad at you. I thought you killed Diamond."

"Hell naw, I had no reason to kill her."

"Cradle said you coulda thought she was talking to the police about what happened."

"Naw, I wouldn't do that, me and Diamond was good. She helped me out in some serious situations. We was like Bonnie and Clyde at one point."

Brittany giggles. "So where you been hiding out at? Where all your clothes and shit at?" she asked, looking at him from head to toe. He wasn't dirty, but she could tell he had worn that outfit for more than one day.

"Shit, I just been buying stuff as the day goes by."

"So what you gonna do? Run forever?"

"Naw, I got a lot of shit to do before I turn myself in. Plus I

know who killed Diamond. I gotta take care of that situation too."

"Oh, I want to meet his ass."

"It's a she and she's white."

"What? A white bitch killed my cousin?"

"Yup, but don't tell anyone."

"I'm not. Who would I tell?"

"Shit, I don't know probably Cradle."

"Fuck Cradle, he wasn't even going to come get me from jail until I told him the address to yo girlfriend's house, Welma or whatever her name is."

"My girlfriend?"

"Yeah that Welma lady, she told on you too. I was about to beat that bitch ass in jail until she called for the guard. When she left, I called Cradle and gave him the address and he said he was going to take care of her so the bitch probably dead," she said.

"Damn, that's fucked up, she deserves to die especially if she told on me," JC said.

"Right but fuck Cradle. I'm not even going to call him. I owe him $1,000, but he not gonna get it."

"You be selling for him?" JC asked.

"Well yeah something like that, but ever since my boyfriend stole a half of a brick from me, Cradle been doing me like I'm just a nigga off the streets. He thinks I had something to do with it or some stupid shit like that. Fuck him."

"It be like that sometimes, so you gone be able to get me a rental car tomorrow?"

"Yeah, I got you. Give me some money too nigga, I ain't about to be paying for everything."

JC laughed, "Girl the money ain't no problem," he said pulling out a wad of money and peeling off $100 for the room and another $300 for the rental car.

"You smoke?" she asked.

"Naw, but the way I've been feeling you can roll that shit up," he said.

CHAPTER 43

"Ok good," she said, pulling some weed out of her pocket. "You done turned bad, you too pretty to be this bad. You look like you should be walking someone's runaway, what happened?"

"Nigga I been like this. I been smoking since I was 12."

"Damn that's crazy. I never woulda thought you was going to be this bad. You know when I use to come around, you was young as hell."

"Well I'm grown now nigga. I'm 17 and I do what I want to do," she said.

JC seen right through her and knew she was led down the wrong path because she thought that it was ok to be the way she turned out. He watched her roll a blunt.

"You got big too. I remember you use to be skinny. You still look like Omarion though," she said, joking with him.

He laughed, "Whatever, you know how to braid?"

"Yeah, I can braid. You ain't heard about me? I'm the coldest on the east. I just stopped because I started getting real money."

"Yeah, I haven't been done up in a minute. I need this shit washed and everything."

"Ok I got you. When we get the rental tomorrow, we can go get all the stuff I need then I'll do you up.

"Shouldn't you be trying to disguise yourself?"

"Girl I'm about to flee the state. I'mma go to Ohio for a minute, I got a cousin out there that's getting money. That's where we going tomorrow."

"Damn nigga you ain't say all that, I got dope to sell," she said, remembering her debt.

"You can sell it when you get there for double."

"For real?"

"Yeah Britt, I told you I got you."

"Alright well we there then."

"I have no choice, I'm definitely not about to get caught trying to be around here when I know it's hot."

"Yeah you right about that."

"I'mma get a fake ID made too, as soon as we get there."

"I want one too."

"You can get one, you probably can pass for about 23 years old," he said.

"I look that old?"

"Naw, but you don't look or carry yourself like you're 17."

"Oh well thanks, I can't wait, you got me geeked now," she said, as she lit the blunt and puffed it a few times then passed it. He was lying on the bed on his back looking up at the ceiling. Brittany was right across from him sitting at the table in the chair.

"You drink too?" she asked.

"Yeah, I fuck with the drink."

She then pulled out two pints of liquor. "I got these on the way up here when we stopped at the store."

CHAPTER 44

"Bet, that works," he said, smiling and puffing the blunt.

Hours later, it was now around 2 o' clock in the morning, and they were talking and getting blowed.

"I remember the time Diamond's boyfriend slapped her. You went over there and tore that boy up with your skinny self. You were skinny and always trying to fight somebody," she said.

He laughed. "Yeah I was a mutha fucka, I use to be bad as hell."

"You still is nigga, you wanted for like 10 murders. You America's Most Wanted and my dumb ass in here drinking and smoking with you. You lucky I got love for you."

He laughed, "They got the wrong dude Britt."

"Shut the fuck up, you did one of them murders, you might not did them all, but you did at least one. Matter fact, I'mma say at least 2."

"Wrong, they got the wrong nigga. They listening to witnesses and in a minute they not gone have any witness. They definitely don't have a gun either. So what do they have?"

"I don't know what they got, but they sound like they got something."

"By the time they get me, if they get me, they won't have no witnesses," he said.

"See listen to you, you're basically saying you gonna get rid of all the witnesses."

"No I'm not," he said, then he bust out in laughter. "I'm high as hell."

"Me too."

They both were up laughing nonstop until 3 o' clock in the morning and they started to get sleepy.

Brittany stripped all the way down to her underwear and got in the bed next to him with an extra sheet.

She was wearing a black bra with see through red boy shorts.

"Damn, what you doing?" JC asked.

CHAPTER 45

"This how I sleep, I can't sleep in jeans."

"Oh ok, don't be doing all that, you got to warn a nigga next time."

She giggled. "Goodnight," she said covering up.

The whole night, she was rubbing her ass against him, but he didn't feed into it. Although he was drunk and high he couldn't get away from what was going on off his mind. Brittany was close all night and she had his dick hard as a rock. They both slept until 10:00 a.m. and Brittany was up first, dressed and on the phone.

She had already taken care of the rental. She was surprised that JC didn't try to have sex with her last night and that made her respect him even more. She went to the store to get the hair supplies, hygiene items, and food for them both. When she came back, JC was wide awoke, and hiding behind the door when she came in.

"Damn JC! You scared the shit out of me!" she shouted, dropping everything she had in her hands.

"My bad, I thought you were with somebody," JC had his guns out and everything, thinking Brittany turned on him or something.

"Nigga, didn't I tell you, you didn't have to worry about me? I'mma loyal bitch. I'm not them hoes you use to fucking with. I'm loyal," she repeated.

"Ok I hear you talking, we will see," he said.

"Here, I got you something to eat. There's a toothbrush and toothpaste in that white bag. I got the car too, it's a Dodge Challenger."

"Damn, you just been up taking care of business huh?"

"That's what I do, I'mma real bitch, you gone see."

He laughed. "You crazy."

"What? I'm serious. Did you want me to get you a outfit to wear today?"

"Naw I'm straight."

"Good, cause I only got me one, but I did get you some boxers. I know them balls sweaty and stinky."

He laughed, chewing on a piece of bacon. "You silly as hell, don't worry about these balls. They can stay sweaty and stinky."

CHAPTER 46

"No they can't, go get in the shower. I'm not about to be riding with you and the whole car stinking."

JC continued to laugh, she had brought his spirit back up. "Ok, I'mma take a shower just for you."

"Thank you."

"How long you pay for the rental for?"

"A week. Is that long enough?"

"Hell naw, we go need it longer than that."

"Well we good. All I gotta do is make a payment online and we can keep it as long as we want."

"Ok cool."

"What kind of guns is them?"

"Stop being nosey," he said

"What's them things on the end?"

"Silencers."

Kelly's phone was ringing off the hook, but it was on vibrate and she couldn't hear anything. Rich had been calling her back to back. Finally, he started calling Marvin."

"Hello." Marvin answered.

"Marvin! Where is Kelly?" Rich asked.

"Who is this?" Marvin asked.

"This is her brother Rich, it's very important. I need to talk to her right now," he said. Marvin could hear the intensity in his voice, but he didn't want to get in their business and ask what was going on."

"Hold on a minute," Marvin said, as he brought the phone to Kelly.

"Hello." Kelly said.

"Sis, you not gonna believe this shit."

"What?"

"We got girls dead and the police been here four times asking questions about a guy named Jason Cakes.

"He used our service and killed a couple girls of ours inside a hotel. Who does that? Now the whole company is been investigated for prostitution!" Rich explained.

"Wait, wait you said Jason Cakes?" she asked stunned.

"Yeah why? You know him?"

"Yeah, I know him. Did they catch him?"

"No, he's on the run."

"Shit! Well close all the houses down and send the girls home. I don't want anyone else coming up dead. You take some money and get out of town, this guy is crazy as hell," Kelly told him.

"Ok sis. When are you coming back?"

"I don't know, call me if you find out anything else."

"Ok I will ok."

Kelly hung up the phone and shook her head in disappointment. Marvin had been listening to the whole conversation. "Jason Cakes? That's JC, I thought you said you finished the job," he said calmly, as he stared her in the face trying to figure her out.

"I thought…I thought I did Marvin," she said.

"Bitch!" he said, as he slapped her and she fell back against the wall.

CHAPTER 47

"Marvin I'm sorry! I thought I finished him!"

"Bitch, you knew! You been acting weird about that dude ever since you claimed you shot him. Something went on with you and him, and I'mma get to the bottom of this," he said, walking out the room. He was pissed.

Kelly was shocked that Marvin hit her. That was the first, but that was nothing compared to what she had just heard from her brother. She went to her phone and saw she had over 70 missed calls. She began returning the calls. First calling her step-dad, Merido.

"Hello, what the hell are you doing not answering the phone?" he asked, as he answered.

"I'm sorry."

"JC is on a rampage, he already made America's Most Wanted. You could be in danger, so can me and your mom. He already struck at your business. Why didn't you finish the job Kelly?

What the hell is wrong with you? This guy is causing all kinds of problems!"

Kelly cried, because she felt like it was all her fault for the murders that were committed. "I don't know what to say," she said, still crying, "I'm sorry."

"Well you need to get your ass back in the states and take care of this maniac. I'm sure the only person he's looking for is you. Why didn't you finish him Kelly? Why would you let him live after you knew what he was doing to all his friends?"

"I…I…I just felt bad, I don't know what I was thinking. I didn't think he would flip out like this," she explained.

"He's all over the news Kelly and he has damn near ten body's they're linking to him."

"Let me figure this out and I'll call you later," she said.

"Bye," he said, hanging up, hoping she knew what the hell she was doing.

"Marvin!" she shouted from the bathroom.

"Fuck you Kelly. If anyone in my family is dead because you didn't finish the damn job, I'mma fuck you up real bad Kelly, I'm not playing."

Kelly could not believe he was snapping on her like this. It was like he turned on her. "Well we can get back at him too. I'm about to make a phone call and make sure his mom dead by the time the sun goes down," she told him as she called a guy she knew that murdered people for money. She gave him the address and the name. He told her he would call her back after he made sure everything was all good.

Three hours later, he called back and told her that his mom was already dead and that she had been shot multiple times. That information turned Kelly's stomach. "This fucker killed his own momma."

"Who, JC?" Marvin asked Kelly.

"Yeah."

"What do you mean killed her?"

"She was found shot multiple times at her home. He's the only person that coulda or woulda done something like that," she said, trying to understand in her own head why he would do that.

CHAPTER 48

"Wow, I can't believe this shit, our kids better be safe and sound. If I make this call and our kids not safe Kelly, I'mma go crazy," he said, as he dialed the number.

"Stop fucking threatening me. What the fuck are you going to do Marvin? You're going to kill me too? Your baby mother huh?"

"Bitch don't tempt me. I just might," he said with a straight face. He wasn't joking at all.

Marvin made the call and told his babysitter to get out of town. The kids were fine and so was the rest of his family. He couldn't understand why JC hadn't got around to his family members yet. But he was glad he hadn't.

"We got to get back to town." Marvin said.

"For what? What are we going to do? We don't know where he could be. We need to stay right here until we can get some kind of tracking on him. You know he won't find us out here," she said.

"We need to find him first."

"Let's just wait Marvin. I don't want nothing to happen to me or you."

———

Rich was scared by the sound of Kelly's voice and he was closing down everything and making plans to get out of town. He called his wife and kids first and told them to go to a house Kelly had and to wait on him. He had no idea that JC and Kelly had met there before. That's the place Kelly was spending the night with JC at, but Rich thought it was safe.

An hour later Rich was opening up the door to the home and was greeted by JC and a bullet to his knee cap. Brittany had his wife and kids tied up and held at gun point. It was broad daylight and JC refused to leave the states without killing one of her family members.

"Where the fuck is your sister?" JC asked, while dragging Rich through the house by his shot leg.

JC and Brittany both had bandanas over their faces. Rich's wife was tied up alone in a black chair, and his two kids were tied up together in the corner. Their legs and hands were tied, and all their mouths had duct tape on them.

"I don't know! Why are you doing this?" Rich asked in pain as he was getting tied up. Blood ran down his leg onto the floor.

"Ask your sister what she did, and then you will understand. Where's the cell phone?"

"In my back pocket…Argh."

CHAPTER 49

B rittany reached in his back pocket and got the cell phone then handed it to JC. Brittany was scared and shaking, but since JC was so calm like he had the situation under control, she was doing the best to stay relaxed.

JC went through his phone and found Kelly's number and he saw Marvin's name as well. He looked at the number and it was the same number for Marvin that Welma had in her phone. "Who the fuck is Marvin?" he asked, hitting Rich in the head with the butt of the gun.

"I don't know what you're talking about," Rich said.

"Boy is you crazy?" Brittany said. "You gone play like you don't know whose number you got in your phone after you heard how many murders this guy has? You better talk!" Brittany shouted.

"I don't know nothing!" Rich shouted.

"You the stupidest guy I ever met Rich. Let me show you what a smart ass mouth to the wrong person can do for you and your family," JC said, raising his gun and shooting his wife in her head.

"Nooooo!" Rich screamed his lungs out, but Brittany quickly covered his mouth with tape.

His kids were in the corner trying to scream, but the tape was on their mouth as well. JC raised his gun up to them next.

Brittany hoped that he didn't and you could see it in her face. She had never seen anything like this in her life. She had no idea JC killed for fun, she was surprised that he still sounded calm and in control. She was praying that JC wouldn't kill the kids next.

"Hmhmmh," Rich was trying to talk so JC pulled the tape off his mouth." It's the father of her kids, her boyfriend!"

JC was shocked. "What? Her boyfriend, baby daddy?"

"Yeah, please don't kill my kids, please!" he pleaded and cried his heart out to JC. "I'm sorry for not answering you! I'll tell you anything you need to know. Just don't kill my kids."

JC called Kelly's phone and it rang twice before she answered. "Hello."

Just hearing her voice pissed him off, but he stayed calm. "I got your brother."

"Who...wh...JC don't do this, keep him out of it!" she said, already knowing JC was going to kill Rich and it was too late.

"I got your niece and nephew too. Hold on, let me let them say hi."

Brittany ripped the tape off their mouths and they both screamed. "Heeeellppp!!!"

"Oh my god, JC please, I'll give you whatever you want. Don't do this. I'll come meet you right now!" She shouted.

He laughed into her ear. "Who did you think you was fucking with? That's what I want to know," he said.

"JC, I'm sorry, someone put me up to this, and I didn't want to do this to you." She said and he could tell she was crying.

"Who put you up to this Marvin?" he asked.

CHAPTER 50

"No, not Marvin."

"Why didn't you tell me about him?"

"JC, it was all about money. I'm sorry," she pleaded for herself, for her family.

"Where's Marvin? Is he right there with you?"

"No, not at this minute. Please don't kill my brother and my niece and nephew. I love them and I'll do whatever you want me to do."

"Well first tell me who put you up to this?"

"Merido."

"Merido?" JC repeated in surprise.

"Yes, he's my step-dad. I guess he did time with you and told you he owns stores or something. I don't know the whole story, but I swear this wasn't my idea. I didn't even want to kill you, that's why I didn't. I knew you coulda been dead, but that was it. I didn't want to kill you JC, please believe me."

JC listened to her cry and actually believed her. He was hurt that Merido was involved. All kinds of things were running through his head and he didn't know what to do. He didn't even know if he still wanted to kill Kelly. He couldn't even speak. All he could think about was when he was just at Merido's store. Merido had played everything cool as if he knew nothing.

"Tell Merido he's dead, and I don't give a fuck. I'm killing you and Marvin as soon as I see you both. Ya'll better find me first," JC said, hanging up in Kelly's face while she was screaming through the phone. He then shot Rich and his kids, and then they both left heading for Ohio.

Cradle, Zip, and Slaps had Welma tied up in an empty room inside one of Cradle's drug houses. They had been shooting her up with Heroin for days now and she kept nodding in and out.

This was the first time Cradle had a chance to talk to her because he had been out of town for a couple days picking up some money.

CHAPTER 51

"**D**amn nigga, we thought you was never gonna come," Slaps said.

Cradle laughed. "Yeah right, where she at?"

"She in the back room," Zip said, as he got off the couch and walked into the room with Cradle. The house had no furniture, but everything had been remodeled. The whole place had tan colored walls with tan carpet to match, which were about two shades darker. It was only a two bedroom home and was in the heart of the hood where people were getting shot and robbed every day.

Cradle opened the room door and saw Welma tied to a chair. She was craving for a hit of Heroin.

"So, tell me about your boyfriend JC," Cradle said.

"Well he's crazy. Can you please give me a fix right now, I need it badly," she said, sweating bullets as the addiction bit into her.

"Yeah, no problem, but first tell me where I can find JC."

"He has no family here in Michigan, but he has some girlfriends, so you might have to find one of them. If I knew anything I would tell you. I'm not trying to die for him. He been left me a long time ago.

"So what the hell you here for? Why ya'll bring this bitch here. She not helpful!" Cradle shouted at his crew.

"You the one told us to go get her, we never even seen this lady," Zip said. Cradle had to stop and think why he had kidnapped Welma. Then it finally clicked. Soon as he remembered he called Brittany.

"Hello."

"Brittany, what you doing?"

"Nothing chillin."

"What's up with this bitch you was in the county jail with?"

"What you mean what's up with her?"

"Why you give me her address and shit?"

CHAPTER 52

"Oh! Because she was telling on her boyfriend for some shit, so I thought she knew something about cuz's murder." Brittany use the word "cuz" because JC was all in her grill wondering who she was on the phone with.

"Do she have something to do with it?" he asked, but got no answer, the phone just hung up. He tried to call back, but the phone just ring and the voicemail just kept picking up. Cradle gave up and walked back to the room.

"What's up, what you find out?" Zip asked.

"The phone went dead, I didn't find out nothing. So there is nothing you can tell me that can help me find JC?"

"Nope, if I knew I would tell you," Welma said.

"Just kill this bitch and get rid of her. Police would think JC did it."

"Wait! Wait! Welma shouted, but Cradle kept walking. He

didn't have time to play games. He knew JC would pop up sooner or later.

———

JC had everybody that was involved in trying to kill him packing up and leaving town because they all were thinking they were going to be next on his list.

Later that night, JC and Brittany arrived in Cincinnati, Ohio. He was nervous about calling his cousin because he hadn't talked to him in so long, but finally he built up the courage to call him.

"Hello.

"Is this Mike?" JC asked.

"Yeah this me, what's hannen? Who this?"

"This your cousin nigga, JC."

"Aww shit, what's up nigga. You been all over the news. What the fuck you got going on? You not in jail are you?"

"Naw, I'm down here with you. I ain't tryna say too much over these punk ass phones though. But can I come through?"

"Can you come through? Yeah you can come through, I ain't seen you since you came home. You remember where the crib at?"

"Oh you still stay there?"

"Naw I don't stay there but I be over there. Meet me there. I'll be there in about ten minutes. You by yourself?" Mike asked.

"Naw I'm with…" He paused and looked over at Brittany then said, "I'm with my girl, she cool."

"Ok, come through."

CHAPTER 53

JC hung up. "Yeah we gonna have to play like we dating down here so this nigga won't think I'm just bringing anyone around him. You cool with that?"

"Yeah, I can do that. I did this before. How old you want me to be?" she asked.

"That's a good question. You can be 19."

"Ok, and how long we been together?" she asked.

"What? That nigga bet not be asking all that shit."

"Just in case he do or someone else do though."

"Damn, you a little thinker. Shit we can say a year."

"Ok."

JC arrived at his cousin's house and noticed Mike had remodeled it. It used to be white, now it was mostly gray with a little white. JC parked in the driveway behind Mike's black

Mercedes 500. JC and Brittany walked up to the door, it was already open and his cousin was standing there holding a stack of money. He threw it at JC who caught it.

"Take that, since I ain't get to see you when you first came home from prison." Mike said, walking towards him. Mike was dressed casual as if he was a businessman. Brown gator shoes, tan slacks, button up shirt and a sweater pulled over it. He and JC hugged each other for the longest. Brittany could tell they had a lot of love for each other.

"Who this?" Mike asked.

"This Brittany, Brittany this is my cousin Mike." They shook hands then all Mike's attention was back to JC.

"What the fuck is going on with you?"

CHAPTER 54

"Man, we gone talk about all that later. I'm tired as hell, I'm trying to get some sleep, but I do need you to tell me where I can go to and be low key. I ain't trying to be around a whole bunch of people," JC said.

"Listen, where you at is safe. This house is up for sale right now. All I gotta do is take the sign down and nobody will be coming over here. There's a bed and shit upstairs where you can sleep at, feel free to stay here man."

"Alright thanks, I really appreciate this."

"No problem, so gone ahead and get settled in. You good at this house, police don't even come on this street."

"Kool."

"I'll be back tomorrow morning to get updated on your situation," Mike said, slapping hands with him before he left out the door.

"He seems cool," Brittany said.

"Yeah, he straight," JC said, walking around the house, checking everything out. "You sleepy?" he asked.

"Hell yeah, I'm going upstairs."

"I'm right behind you," JC said.

When they got upstairs to the room and opened the door, they saw only a twin size bed sitting in the middle of the floor with one sheet on there that had over a 100 nut stains all over it.

"Ughh!" Brittany said.

JC started laughing. "This nigga crazy, he must be fucking his lil females over here."

"Clearly."

CHAPTER 55

"Well, all we gotta do is flip the mattress over and find another sheet," he said.

They couldn't find any sheets, so JC called Mike and was told that there were plenty of sheets in a closet downstairs. Brittany found them and made the bed. She then began stripping down to her tan bra and tan boy shorts.

"This a twin size bed, you can't sleep like that Brittany."

"Why?" she asked with a smirk.

"Because it ain't no room for me unless I'm right on your ass."

"You'll be ok," she said smiling while getting under the sheet.

JC already knew she wanted him to have sex with her, but he wasn't trying to go there with her. He thought about sleeping on the floor, but he didn't want to piss her off, especially after what she had just seen him do. He was starting to think that having sex with her is what he might have to start doing. JC took off all his clothes and got in the bed with her, wearing just a pair of boxers and a white tank top. They were extra close to one another because the bed was so little. To keep from getting hard, JC turned the opposite way and began trying to fall asleep. About ten minutes later, Brittany felt his dick on her booty. She had to feel it to even believe that what she was feeling was really his dick. She grabbed it gently and JC didn't move. He was snoring, she kept feeling it from the bottom all the way up.

"JC," she whispered into his face. The light was still on in the room and Brittany could see that JC was in a deep sleep. She slowly raised the covers up to look at his dick, because she had never had anything inside her that big. The five guys she had dealt with were five inches or smaller and JC was double that. "JC," she whispered again.

"Mmmhh," he mumbled in his sleep.

"Good night," she whispered, wanting to kiss him on his soft lips but she didn't.

"Mmm hmm," he moaned back.

Brittany was horny, but sleepier from the long drive. She got out the bed, turned off the light then laid back under JC with his arm around her. She slept all night while his dick was constantly hard against her petite body. The next morning, JC was up bright and early. His cousin had arrived at around 7 a.m. and they were both downstairs having breakfast while Brittany was still sleeping.

"So tell me what happened. They got you on the news talking about you killed all kinds of people. What's hannen?" Mike asked, as he sat across the table from JC.

"To be honest, I'mma just tell you everything from the

beginning. Then you tell me if I'm crazy or did some crazy shit happen to me?"

Mike laughed. "Oh, we already established you crazy. That's a fact," he said joking. They both started laughing.

"Naw but, as you know, I went to prison for a little bit."

"Right."

CHAPTER 56

" While I was down, I was kicking it with this one dude. He's a foreign guy named Merido. We became friends and he was telling me all about the franchise game. He told me how I can franchise a convenience store for like 300 hundred thousand, but I'll make the money right back, plus some.

"Damn, he was out there getting money like that?" Mike asked.

"Yeah, he still is, he out, but dig how he played me."

"Ok, I'm listening."

"Me and this dude was extra cool. I'm talking about we use to fight together and everything.

He was my bunky for like a year, you know?"

"Ok, what he do?"

"I got out first and I was fucking with Rita, remember her?"

"Yeah I remember Rita. How she doing?"

"She dead, but anyways, I was--"

"She dead? How she die nigga?"

"I'mma get to that, let me tell the story."

"Alright nigga tell the story."

"I came home to her, she wasn't talking about shit, so I bust up on her after I started meeting all these older hoes on that internet shit that was willing to cash a nigga out. So I left Rita and got with this older lady name Welma. She was balling. I'm talking Condo, Lexus and Beamer, paid for. Balling, you feel me?"

"Hell yeah, I woulda left her ass too," Mike said.

"Right, so you know I hooked up with her and shit, got job and was stacking my money for a minute.

CHAPTER 57

"You know I get checks automatically for having Cherokee in me. So I'm stacking my money. Ok remember all the niggas I used to hang with when I used to get money before I went to prison?"

"Umm, who you talking about, Chip, Dre and the rest of them?"

"Yeah, I get out of prison on some straight wild shit, like I'm robbing all these niggas. So I start having this ill bitch setting all them up. I'm hitting these niggas for stupid thousands of dollars, you hear me Mike?"

Mike smiled as he watched JC starting to really get into his story. "Right."

"I'm talking I'm hitting they ass for 30 and 40 thousand. These dudes were really getting a little money out there. The reason why I robbed them though is because when I was doing my time they didn't send me nothing or send a letter. I mean they showed me no love. So I robbed all of them."

"Damn."

"Yeah, but anyway, I met a white girl online. I started kicking it with her. I leave Welma for her, move in with her and everything, and come to find out she got a man and kids, plus she Merido step-daughter. The dude I was just telling you about."

"She his stepdaughter?"

"Yeah."

"And?"

"The bitch tried to kill me. The whole thing was a set up. Merido had to have told this hoe about me. So she played me like she was single, no kids, and all, then when I had enough money to buy the store he tried to kill me for damn near two hundred thousand. The bitch shot my shoulder all up and shit," JC said, showing Mike the bullet scar. "She shot me twice but the bullet went right through. I got shot in the same arm and in the leg too, but I'm good. I went to the hospital, they performed emergency surgery on me, and I wind up running away from there because the police was trying to charge me with some murders. All the new shit I've been doing is because I'm trying to find that white bitch Kelly. That bitch got my money."

CHAPTER 58

"So, you telling me, you let a dude you was in prison with set you up?"

"Something like that. So far I got to Kelly's brother and his family, but I have yet to see her. They got me good. They even paid the older bitch I was with to put cameras in the house, so they saw every time I came in with some money. They knew everything about me and I had no clue."

"The older bitch was involved too?"

"Naw, not like that. She say the dude was acting as if he was a detective or some shit. I guess he showed her all kinds of paper work and she fell for it, but not only did she fall for that she was fucking him too. Man, shit has been all fucked up."

"That's some crazy shit. I couldn't imagine going through some shit like that. So what happened to Rita?" JC smiled and shook his head. "She had to go dog. She was gonna be a problem with what I was trying to do."

"So they trying to charge you with her murder too?"

"I don't know what they trying to do. I ain't going to jail until Merido, Kelly, and Kelly's boyfriend is dead, and that's real talk."

Mike could see that JC was serious and for no games. "Well I don't know how long you gonna be around before you have to deal with all that shit you facing, but I know what you need to be doing right now, and that's making as much money as you can for a good ass lawyer."

CHAPTER 59

"Shit well you the man in Ohio. What you got for me to do? I murder, torture, and I'll sell a lil dope if I have to."

"What about home girl you with?"

"She with me, she on the same tip," JC said.

"You know bitches get in the way sometimes?"

"Hell yeah I know. That's why if she do anything out of the ordinary she'll be gone too. Listen Mike, I ain't playing no games out here. Kids getting it too."

"Damn I miss doing all that crazy shit. You know I use to be a rampage back in the day until they gave me those 15 years. Luckily I got that shit overturned and only came out with five and manslaughter."

"Oh I know, I heard how you used to get down. You still do on the low, you probably just smarter," JC said. He knew Mike was a real killer and had gotten away with plenty of murders in his past. Mike use to be a gangsta but he changed his life after doing five years, and now he's getting money in the corporate world. Plus, moving drugs in and out of state.

"Naw, I don't fuck around no more, I got too much to lose now. I have kids and a wife now. So now I got a team of goons and goonettes that handle all that for me."

"Well let me get all them jobs, I need that money right now."

"Ok, but first, I'mma hook up with my guy that can give you and your girl a whole new identity. I'm talking about birth certificates and everything, and it's all legit. You won't ever see any of them charges unless you fuck the new identity up and they get your DNA or fingerprints. By the time he gets all your new paperwork, you would have been made a nice amount of money then you can invest in some bricks I'm getting for you and who whatever else. But just make sure under this new identity you do not put yourself in a position where you can go to jail because that's when they gone try to hammer your ass. They gone bring all them murders up when they find out who you really is."

"Ok, I can do this, it's nothing."

"Ok, I got this one dude in Columbus, a city not too far from here. He owes me 2.3 million. I need you to see what's going on he haven't answered in two weeks or called. He has surveillance around the whole house. So you gonna have to follow his wife, his son, or him when they leave the house. Depending on how good you do on this, I'll tear you off real nice."

"Damn big cuz, you in Ohio doing it like this?" Why you ain't call me to come down here a long time ago?"

"Man I tried to reach out to you, but you was hard to find, don't get it twisted I'm a middle man so even though I'm dealing with millions that doesn't necessary mean I have millions of dollars."

CHAPTER 60

"Well do you?"

Mike laughed. "I mean, my net worth about 4 million, but I'm telling you that for future reference. You can be transferring millions, but you don't have one million. That's because a lot of other people have to get paid besides you."

"Oh ok, because I was just thinking like if I go get 2.3 million, I better get at least 500 thousand."

"Damn, that's not even my profit!" Mike said.

"Well, I'm glad you explained that because we probably woulda fell out just over that."

"Listen JC, I been knowing you since you came on this earth. I'm not gone ever cheat you, and I would hope you will never cheat me. Just let me show you how this shit is going and when you get your money, you're free to do your own thing. Deal?"

"Alright. So what if dude don't have the money?"

"He will. If not all he will have something. I don't too much believe in just killing people no more because all that means is I get nothing. I would rather take a finger or two first, maybe a few toes."

JC made a nasty looking face but started laughing. "I thought I was sick, but damn, you really out cold with your shit, doing some Hannibal Lector stuff."

"It's just business though JC. That shit happens in the corporate world too. In fact it's really no different besides you not having to watch out for the police anymore."

"Damn that's crazy."

"It's reality."

Brittany came walking in on them. "Where mine at? I'm hungry too," she said.

"Here you can have this, I ain't gone eat it," JC said and Brittany came over and sat on his lap and started eating. She was always surprising JC with the things she did but he didn't mind.

"Well, I'm about to get out of here. Here the map to dudes house and here's directions to where all the stores at where you can go shopping for the house and yourself. Oh and your girl here. Ya'll make ya'll selves at home. Ya'll safe here, believe that."

"Thanks cuz, I really appreciate you looking out for me, knowing what I'm up against. That's love."

CHAPTER 61

"Don't trip, you my people, plus I know what you going through right now. I've been there and nobody was there for me. Our own family members closed the door in my face when I tried to come to their house while I was on the run."

"Well good looking. I'mma take care of this and I'll holla at you later," After Mike left, JC and Brittany was still sitting at the table.

Brittany was still sitting on his lap eating the rest of the food. "That shit good or something?" said JC.

Brittany giggled while chewing her food, "It is, here taste," she said, dipping her fork in the hash brown and eggs then feeding it to JC.

"Mmm, that is good. Give me some more."

She giggled again, "I told you," she said smiling and feeding him.

"Why you come downstairs like that?" JC asked her.

"What's the big deal?" she asked?"

"You forgot already? We supposed to be together. You think if you was really my girl, I would let you come around me and someone else like this?"

"Oh, I'm sorry. I didn't think nothing of it because this is more of a sports bra. I can wear this by itself if I wanted to. Look, it's not see through or nothing."

"Oh, I'm tripping, you right that ain't shit. I'm just looking at it from the back. You straight though."

"Don't worry I'm not gone embarrass you."

He started laughing.

"So what's up, what your cousin talking about?" she asked, turning to look at him.

"Really nothing. He has a job for us to do though. I was mainly telling him what's going on with the whole situation."

"What kind of job?"

"Somebody owe him some money, he wants me to go get it."

"Or make dude pay."

"Yeah I don't think I'll be killing nobody."

"Good, that shit is too scary I was shaking for so long yesterday."

JC smiled, "That's normal. I used to shake too. Now it's nothing."

Brittany didn't understand how it could be so easy for JC to take someone's life, but she liked the fact that he didn't play games. She hated punks and guys that let women run over them. She could already tell that JC was probably not the one to try and regulate.

"You was knocked out last night. I was messing with you and didn't even move."

"Don't be messing with me while I'm sleep. What was you doing?"

"Trying to move your big thang out the way. It was hard all night. What you was thinking about while you was sleep?" she said, turning to look at him with a grin on her face.

JC laughed first before he said, "Don't be doing that while I'm sleep, I'mma start sleeping on the floor in a minute."

CHAPTER 62

S he giggled, "And I'mma be on the floor right with you."

They both started laughing and she continued to eat and feed him.

JC liked the way she showed affection towards him. Although they wasn't dating or having sex just being around the two of them you would think they were together or sex buddies.

"I need to get some clothes. You want to go shopping?" JC asked.

"Let's go. I hope you got some money for me too."

"You know I got you."

"I won't hit them pockets too hard. I can be a girly girl when it comes to dressing."

"Good," he said patting her thigh so she could get up off him. "Finish getting dressed," he told her.

They spent a couple of hours at the grocery and clothing store. JC wasn't trying to spend much money so he bought a lot of white beaters and white tee's along with six pair of pants. She even bought several pair of underwear.

On the way home they stopped at the dollar store and they both went in and bought some things. JC felt comfortable because he was out of state and no one knew him. Of course his face was on the news. But the picture they had of him didn't really resemble the way he looked now. Their picture was old.

Walking to the register, Brittany picked up a box of condoms.

"What's that for?" JC asked.

"For my needs. You not about to have me way down here doing favors and not giving me no dick. What you think this is? I got needs too nigga," she said, looking at him like he was crazy, but all he could do was smile and laugh at her.

"You silly." Was all he could say because he knew she was right.

"Can you even fit these?" she asked holding up the box.

He shook his head no.

"What about these?" she asked holding up the black and gold box.

He shook his head yes and smiled.

"You got everything?" she asked

"Yeah, I'll be in the car. I'm about to drive up to the door."

CHAPTER 63

"Okay."

They drove back to where they were staying and Brittany took a bath downstairs and JC took one upstairs. After eating again, it was around seven at night and the sun was going down, so JC decided to drive out to the guy's house that owed Mike some money.

"Damn, who house is this?" Brittany asked.

"This the house we gonna have to stake out at for a lil while. It shouldn't be long. The first person that leaves we gone snatch up. But right now, we gonna park right here and relax. Keep our eyes open."

"Ok, that works for me. You know what I'm bout to do right?"

"What?"

"Smoke and pop this bottle open," she said.

"I'm with you," he said, arriving at a driveway that no one lived at. The house was for sale and it had no blinds up. It wasn't too far from the target and they were able to see the driveway perfectly.

"What's this guy name?" she asked.

"Danny, that's what it says on this paper."

"Well what you want me to do? What's the plan?"

"Just follow my lead, let me do the talking."

"Ok," she said, rolling up a fat blunt of weed.

"I'm not tryna smoke, but I'll have a drink or two."

"More for me!" she said.

Eight o'clock came and JC had his seat laid back. He was buzzing off the liquor. Brittany was a little drunk and she was high as hell. She kept smiling and looking over at JC until he said, "What you keep looking at me smiling for?"

"Because it's funny right now."

"What's funny right now?"

"You and me together chilling."

"What that mean?"

"I just never thought this day would ever happen. I remember when I used to be super young and I was so in love with you. Every time I used to see you with Diamond, I would try and show off."

"You silly."

"For real, I had a major crush on you," she said, giggling again.

"Why you laughing?"

"I'm laughing because I'm high as hell, but the other reason is because you so cute. Every time I look at you I just can't stop smiling."

"Thank you, with your silly ass."

"Ok let me stop. I am high right now though, you shoulda hit that. It was some fire. I got that from my cousin."

"So you cool being all the way out here with me?" he asked.

"Yeah, I'm cool with this. Why you asked that?"

"I'm just making sure because I kind of snatched you up not knowing whether or not you had a lot of things going on there."

CHAPTER 64

"No, I'm good. You good, I'm happy to be with you honestly. I'd say you have perfect timing."

"Just checking."

"Your girlfriend was ugly and old looking. What's wrong with you?"

"What girlfriend?" he asked laughing.

"Welma."

"That ain't my girlfriend, she just used to give me money and shit."

"Oh, I was about to say."

"What was you about to say?"

"You too cute for the lady. You need to be with a cute girl like me."

He laughed, Brittany wasn't scared to speak her mind at all. He liked that about her.

"A girl like you? What can you do for me that she couldn't do?"

"A lot! She can't dance, fuck you or suck your dick like I would."

"See, that's where you getting it fucked up at. Other dudes may care about that type of shit, whether a female can fuck, suck or dance. But me, I want a female with a big bank account. That pretty shit means nothing to a nigga like me."

Brittany could not believe what she was hearing. A guy never said anything like that to her. She barely knew how to respond to something like that. "So what you saying, you a gold digger?"

"Naw, I show my women major love. I treat them good. I eat that pussy and lay that dick the way they like it, but this here ain't for free."

"What? So you don't fuck for free?"

He laughed, "See now you jumping to some whole other shit. I'm talking about the women I deal with repeatedly."

"So what will I have to do to have you?"

He looked at her and was shocked but said, "Just do you."

"Just do me? Tell me what you like."

"I just did."

"So I just have to have some money?"

He laughed, "Come on Brittany don't take me through all this tonight."

"Well tell me nigga," she said, socking him in his chest.

"I'll tell you later."

CHAPTER 65

"You full of shit. Well what I gotta do for you to give me some dick?"

JC turned and looked at her to see if she was serious. He thought she was joking, but she was dead ass serious. "Not much."

"Well what?" she asked, biting her bottom lip. "What if I wanted to give you some head right now? What would you say?"

"I wouldn't say nothing, I'll just pull my dick out and let you suck it."

"Pull it out then," she said, pulling her hair back in a ponytail and pushing the seat back.

JC unzipped his pants while he was lying back, and then pulled them down. His dick was standing straight up. Brittany went right for it, first kissing on the head of it then working her way all the way down to his balls then back up with her tongue. "You like that?"

"Yeah, that feels good, put it in your mouth," he instructed her.

"Put it in my mouth?" she said before she stuck his whole dick half way down her throat and kept it there until she felt him grab her hair and pull it.

"Ohh shit!" he whispered. "Keep going," he said and Brittany continued. She was able to deep throat so good, JC fell in love with the way she sucked his dick. She kept deep throating, stroking his dick with her hand and popping her lips on the head of his dick. That drove him crazy. Brittany kept her head bobbing up and down while her hand stroked his dick all in the same motion. She knew she was sucking his dick good because she heard him moaning. Plus she had his body jerking nonstop and he hadn't even nutted yet. She had his dick swelled up even bigger. That's when she knew he was about to cum, so she put the whole thing in her throat and JC went crazy. He could barely take it.

"Britt…any!" he screamed like a girl as he was holding on to her head with both of his hands when he came down her throat. She felt him squeezing both sides of her head. She didn't mind swallowing every drop of him. Even when JC had let his last drop fall down her throat, she still had his whole dick in her mouth and JC wondered if she was even able to breathe. He couldn't believe the way she handled his dick because she was so little. After pulling his dick out her mouth he couldn't help but ask, "How the hell you put this whole dick in your mouth? My dick damn near bigger than your whole face."

She laughed, "Yeah, it's big, but I don't know. I use to sneak and watch Super head DVDs all the time, so I guess you can say I got it from her."

"Damn, that shit was good as hell!" he said, as he buttoned his pants back up. He wanted to tell her that she was the best he ever had, but he didn't. "I don't normally cum when a female suck my dick, but damn!"

Brittany was just smiling and laughing. She appreciated that he loved the head that she had just gave him.

"I want that shit every morning when you wake up. You don't even have to wake me up, just start sucking." Brittany was already pretty to him and having good pussy, good head, and being a squirter made things much better for him. He started liking her even more. He was ready to leave the sight they were at just to go home and fuck her.

"Is that pussy as good as your head game?"

"its better, you want to taste it?"

"Hell yea, why not?"

CHAPTER 66

B rittany took her pants off and pushed her seat all the way back. JC helped her as he sucked and kissed around her titties all the way down to her panty line. He used his teeth to pull her soaking wet panties off then used his tongue all the way back up from her ankle and licked right between her thighs. Brittany was already soaking and wet before she dropped her panties and now she was dripping juices all over the seat. She had nutted in her panties just off the fact of how turned on she was. JC climbed over to her seat and was on his knees with her pussy lips spread as far apart as possible while he was licking and sucking her clit with all he had.

"Ooohh, J!" she screamed, bumping her pussy off and on his tongue. "Fu….c.k!"

JC continued licking now sticking two fingers in and out of her pussy. It wasn't long before she started shaking like crazy then squirting all over his face. He swallowed as much as he could, but she had come so much, it was all over the place. He had to move his face out the way because she was squirting so much she probably could've drown him.

"Damn baby," he said, as he worked his fingers inside her. Her pussy was soaking wet. "Your pussy wet as hell," he said, as he stared at her while she was still moaning and trying to catch her breathe.

"It's.. Always…like…this," she said in between breathes.

Finally JC pulled his fingers out her pussy. He had white creamy cum all over his hand and it was leaking on the seat she was sitting in. "Damn, look at all this shit. This normal for you?" he asked.

She smiled. "Yeah, I got that Aquafina flow for real, don't I?"

He laughed. "You think you the shit, don't you?"

"Nooo, I just know my pussy good."

"How you know that? I don't know yet. You taste good though and I like how wet and creamy you get. So when we get to the spot, I'mma see how good that pussy really is."

"I can't wait!" she said, trying to wipe her cum off the seat and off her thighs. "Damn, I nutted a lot, look it's still coming out."

"What my pussy taste like?"

"It didn't taste like nothing. It taste fresh, it taste like water."

CHAPTER 67

"It tastes good? Would you eat it again?"

"Hell yeah, I'll eat that pussy all night, literally."

She smiled, "You silly, let's go we can come back tomorrow."

"Naw, as bad as I want to go, I need this money. Just chill with me ok."

"Ok, but I'm about to smoke again."

"Go ahead."

Brittany started smoking another blunt and this time JC smoked with her. It wasn't long before the blunt was gone and Brittany was all over JC kissing his lips, face and neck, "Let's do it," she whispered in his ear, as she straddled him in the driver's seat. After he gave her the ok, that's when they both went crazy on each other and started having hot, rough, and sweaty sex. Brittany had bit him all over the lower part of his neck and the top part of his chest. She couldn't help herself because she was in so much pain and pleasure. They had sex for hours nice and slow and JC had cum inside her twice and Brittany came three times. They started having sex in the driver seat then it went to the passenger seat then to the back where he was on top of her stroking her nice and slowly.

They both were all sticky and smelled like sex as they laid on top of each other in the back seat. JC was still inside her and she was still soaking wet. It was like her pussy never stopped dripping wet. This was by far the wettest pussy JC had ever had and it was good. Brittany finally raised her head up off his shoulder and JC noticed he had blood on his stomach. "What the fuck is this? You on your period?"

CHAPTER 68

"No, you just popped my cherry," she admitted lying her head back on his shoulder, embarrassed.

"Say you swear."

"I swear."

"Your cherry ain't never been popped?" he asked surprised.

"No."

"You just full of surprises. You den nutted all over the car, now you bleeding on me," he said, just messing with her.

Brittany couldn't stop laughing. She knew JC liked it, but she also knew he was drunk which enhanced everything.

"I know, I'm sorry," she whined and kissed his neck.

He was still on hard and still inside her. "You ready to go? Because I need to get in the shower.

I'm all sticky."

"Wait. I don't want to get off of you yet."

"It feels good?"

She blushed, "Hell yeah."

She sat there for about ten more minutes, JC got him another nut off. They both got dressed the best they could then started the car up, defrosted the window and drove back to where they were staying. "Okay we got to hurry up because I'm trying to go right back over there," JC said, looking at the time. It was 5:45 a.m. They took a shower together and Brittany couldn't keep her hands off JC. She made him fuck her in the shower also. Their shower only lasted about 25 minutes. They then headed back to where they were and waited a little longer.

Around 8:30 a.m, a silver Range Rover was pulling out of the driveway. JC couldn't tell who was in it because the windows were tinted, so he started following the vehicle.

"We got action," he said, driving behind another car that was in back of the Range Rover.

Brittany was getting JC's gun ready for him, checking to make sure that it was cocked and loaded.

"This one all set to go," she said, setting on his lap.

CHAPTER 69

J C was trying to focus on not getting too close and being seen. They drove about ten minutes before the Range Rover turned into a gas station to get some gas. JC kept going but turned into a bank parking lot next door where he was able to see the person that was driving the Range Rover.

"Oh, it's two of them in the car," JC said.

"Is that him?"

"Naw, that gotta be his son he was telling me about. The girl must be his girlfriend or something," JC said, as he still stared at both of them as they walked back to the vehicle.

"Let's see where they go."

JC watched them fill up then began following them again to a neighborhood that had a rich vibe to it. JC watched the Range Rover pull in front of a house. The girl got out and went inside then the driver did a U-turn in the middle of the street only to be blocked by the car that JC and Brittany were in.

They got out quickly, pointing their guns at him. JC ran up on the car while Brittany stood back pointing her gun.

"Get the fuck out!" JC said, breaking the window with his gun and snatching him out and hitting him with his gun a few times. JC patted him down quickly for a weapon, but all he had was a pocket knife and a wad of money.

"Chill," the victim screamed.

Brittany still had her gun pointed, but she was starting to get scared because she felt that JC wasn't moving fast enough. It was broad daylight outside. She took it upon herself to open the trunk, so that JC could throw him in there after beating him unconscious.

Then Brittany jumped inside the Range Rover as instructed by JC and followed him to a big parking lot where they parked the Range Rover and left it there. Brittany then got back in the car with JC and they drove until they heard the dude in the trunk wake up.

"Please, let me out of here!" he shouted, banging on the trunk.

"I will, but first tell me a few things," JC shouted back.

Brittany looked in the back seat and seen that there was an arm rest that came down in the middle which also had a small piece that came off, so that the inside of the trunk could be seen.

She climbed in the back to set things up, so that they could hear each other. "You try anything crazy, I'mma pop your ass right from this hole," she said, pointing her gun at him.

"What you want to know?" he asked.

CHAPTER 70

"What's your name and how old are you?"

"Danny and I'm 24."

"You Danny? What, Danny Jr.?"

"Yeah. My dad is Big Danny."

"Which one of ya'll owes Mike some money?" JC asked.

"That's my dad. I have nothing to do with that. I'm a college student at Ohio University."

"So, where is your dad?"

"He's out of town right now."

"What are you doing at his house?"

"I live there. What do you mean?"

"Well, tell him if he don't have Mike's money, I'mma kill you, him and your mom. Then I'mma kill the lil hoe you just dropped off."

"Ok, I'll tell him as soon as I talk to him."

"You play with me, I will find you again and next time I won't be so nice."

"Me neither," Brittany said, still pointing her gun at the hole.

"Ok, Ok. No problem. I can't guarantee anything though," Danny said and that pissed JC off. He now felt as if Danny was taking him as a joke.

"Shoot him B."

"Huh?"

"Pop his ass!"

"Where? I can't see where I'm shooting," she said.

"So what, just pull the trigger!" JC shouted.

"No! Please! No! Aghhh!" he said as he caught a bullet in his hand. "Oww! My hand! Get me to a hospital!" he said, crying and shouting.

CHAPTER 71

"Now, like I said before, make sure your dad pays or next time I won't be so nice," JC said, as he stopped the car on the side of the street where no cars were in sight. He hopped out and opened the trunk to let Danny out. Danny was bloodied and bruised all over his face. JC threw him on the side of the road and sped off.

"Good job. I was hoping you hit him somewhere like the hand or leg. I didn't want to kill him. I just wanted to scare the shit out of him."

"I couldn't see shit back there."

"Well, that was a lucky ass shot."

"Thanks," she smiled and climbed back in the front seat. They drove back to where they were staying and waited until Mike called. By the time he called it was 3 p.m. and Brittany had just finished washing and braiding JC's hair.

"Hello," JC answered.

"What's up? You don't even have to say anything. Danny called me and told me he was going to get the money to me later on. I'll drop you off $15,000. I appreciate what you did too."

"No problem."

"I got another name for you too, but this will be a smaller and much easier job."

"Ok, well I'll be at the spot with B chilling."

JC hung up and was a little angry about only getting $15,000. He didn't say anything though because he was thinking things will get better. Fifteen thousand was better than what he had right now. JC was planning on doing one more job for him to make a little more money than he planned on buying a kilo of cocaine with his money. Mike came over around seven that evening to cash JC out and tell him about another job. He told him he only gave him $15,000 because he didn't have to murder anyone. JC eventually understood.

After Mike left, JC was upstairs lying on the bed in deep thought about everything until Brittany came in.

"We got $21,848. I counted that shit like three times."

"Ok. After this job, we gone buy a kilo and hit the block," he said.

CHAPTER 72

"Ok. I'm with you baby," she said, walking over to him and kissing him on the lips.

---

2 months later

Stone was lying on his bunk when he got an envelope and a money receipt from the correctional officer. It was a letter from Ohio and the name on it wasn't familiar.

"Who is this?" Stone said as he quickly started reading the letter.

What's good? You thought I forgot about you didn't you? Well I haven't. Although, they say I'm wanted, I don't feel wanted. I'm doing good now. A lot of shit hit the fan, but it's nothing. You just make sure you take care of yourself in there. I sent you a $500 money order and I'll send you $100 every week, so *you can do what you want to in that bitch. I know it's fucked up for you in there, but I got you until they take me out and that's my word. I'm sorry about Tia. I know you had a lot of love for her, but shit happens. Just make sure you not believing what the news and shit saying. It wasn't who they say it was. Oh, I got a seed on the way too. I went on and put one in this new female I got on my team. She real loyal and bout what I'm bout. Every man dream, you feel me? I don't know if it's a boy or a girl yet, but I'll let you know when I find out. But anyways, I'm just showing you some love. Everything good this way. I was going to use that Jpay shit, but I said fuck it and let my girl write you while I talked lol. But I probably won't write no more, but the money will be there every week. Holla at me at the P.O box listed below. Be easy. JC.*

Stone finished reading the letter and was a happy to get the letter from JC, he had thought JC was dead or in the Feds. Stone was also happy to receive some money. None of his people had been showing him love for the past six months.

CHAPTER 73

"Look, my nigga sent a nigga five hundred like it's nothing!" Stone said to his bunky.

"Who that? The dude you was telling me about, with all the hoes?"

"Yeah, this nigga say he doing good and he got a shorty on the way!"

"He ain't send you no pictures?"

"Naw, this nigga ain't about to take no pictures." Stone said.

He was thankful for the money JC sent. Now he was able to eat much better because they fed you like a kid in prison. If a person's family wasn't sending money, that prisoner has a hard fight making it through his time. Of course there were little hustles, but when a guy's trying to go home, he's not trying to be stabbing or beating somebody up over a few noodles.

Mike was on his way to meet his connect where he got all his cocaine from. He was driving a new Chrysler Van, riding with his sideline female he had been dealing with for years now. Her name was Shawna. An Albino with long curly blonde hair. She was so in love with Mike and was the only woman who loved his belly. She loved fat guys because they were so soft to her.

Mike finally arrived at the spot, but his connect was not there. This was unusual because he was always on time.

"Where is he?" Shawna asked.

"I don't know," Mike said, as he looked around. It was daylight, so it wouldn't be hard to see him if he was near but Mike didn't see him nowhere.

"Call him," Shawna said.

Mike did just that.

"Hello," a voice answered.

"Hello, Temple?" Mike asked.

"Yeah this Temple," a voice said, but the voice didn't sound familiar at all to Mike, so he hung up and drove off as fast as he could.

"What's wrong?" Shawna said, as her eyes grew big as apples as his speed accelerated.

"Either the police just answered his phone or he lost it. It had to be the police because we always meet here, same time every Thursday, no matter what!"

Shawna was listening before she said, "Call one of the other guys he deals with and see if they've heard from him."

Mike picked up his phone and the first person he called was Cradle.

"Hello."

"Cradle, what's up? This Mike."

"What's up Mike? I already know why you calling. Temple got hit and the state got him on a punk ass pistol charge."

"Damn man, so what's up, is he gonna be working?"

"Not no time soon."

"Damn, did you get to meet him?"

"Yup, he just hit me with 70 of them too."

CHAPTER 74

"Damn! Well how much you gone charge me for like 10? I got somebody that's been waiting for two weeks now," Mike said.

"Man, I gotta have 18 a piece."

"Come on man! You just gone tax me like that!" Mike shouted.

"Man, I gotta have that. I'm getting 22 for each one all day right now. It's dry out here in these streets. I should be charging more than that. Niggas around this bitch selling bricks for 30, and you crying about 18. You got shit fucked up!"

"Man, I get the same ticket you get though, Cradle."

"You can pay an extra $4,000. I gotta make something off you. I know you about to go give it to your people for at least 25," Cradle said.

"Hell naw, I don't be taxing like that. I'm Mr. Wholesale."

"I know you seen your stupid ass cousin on the news," Cradle said.

"Yeah, but I ain't trying to talk about that nigga. You know I ain't got nothing to do with that shit."

"Shit, you can have all ten of these bricks if you tell me where that nigga at," Cradle said.

Mike froze up and was quiet. He looked over at Shawna then back at the road.

"Say what?"

"I'll give you all ten, if you tell me where your cousin at."

"Where do I have to come and get them?" Mike asked.

"Detroit. You know where I be at. Come through." Cradle said before he hung up the phone.

Mike put his phone down slowly and was thinking about what he was about to do. That was a lot of money for his cousin. He didn't even think JC was worth that much, but people really wanted him dead.

"What he say?" Shawna asked.

"We gotta go to Detroit to get them."

"He taxing you a lot?"

Mike shook his head, "Naw, it's all good."

Cradle called Kelly as soon as he hung up with Mike.

"Hello," Kelly answered.

"Is this Kelly?" Cradle asked.

"Yes, this is her. Who is this?"

"This is Cradle, the dude that bought the convenience store from your stepdad."

"Oh, hi. What's happening?"

CHAPTER 75

"Well our first encounter seemed to go well, although it seemed like it was more about JC. I don't know exactly what went on with all, but I remember you saying you'd spend a hundred thousand to find him."

"Yeah, he killed my brother. Where you at right now? Maybe we can meet each other or something and talk more," she said.

"Ok." Cradle told her where to meet him.

Cradle and Kelly hung up and met later on. Kelly told him that she would have Marvin drop the money off to him later when Cradle found out exactly where JC was living. They talked about everything and shared stories about how bad they wanted JC. They finally came to an agreement that both of them would get a piece of him no matter what. Kelly wanted a piece of him and so did Cradle. Kelly even cried and told Cradle how JC killed her brother's entire family with her on the line listening. Kelly was so hurt, she hated JC's guts. She wanted him to suffer and shooting him wasn't enough. That wouldn't satisfy her.

Cradle assured her that he would let her do anything she wanted to JC before he blew his head off. Cradle still had no idea that JC had gotten Brittany pregnant. Brittany would talk to Cradle every now and then, but she never mentioned anything about JC. All she did was pay her debt with Cradle and made sure he was never coming near her or JC.

Brittany was basically keeping a tab on Cradle for JC and steering him in the wrong direction.

She still didn't believe that JC killed her cousin Diamond and there wasn't anyone that could make her believe the rumor. She fell in love with JC and now she felt in her heart that she had to protect him from any harm.

Kelly trusted Cradle because they shared almost the same experience. They planned to meet up one more time after he got the money to discuss when and where everything was going to take place. Kelly left happy as ever and all Cradle was thinking about when he left Kelly was how big her ass and hips were. He wanted to have sex with her, so bad and he was hoping she would give him some along with the hundred grand.

When Kelly left, she went straight to where Marvin had a suite at. She couldn't wait to tell him the good news.

"Baby, guess what?" Kelly said.

"What?" he asked, as he watched her walk in wearing a white dress that she looked like she was about to bust out of.

"We're about find JC. All you have to do is bring the money to this address as soon as possible then he's gonna give you the address to where JC is."

"This is the same guy that bought Merido's store right?"

"Yeah, he good," Kelly said.

CHAPTER 76

"Good, I can't wait to see JC. He been running for a while now," Marvin said, hugging and grabbing Kelly's booty. They kissed and he started pulling her dress up noticing she wasn't wearing any panties. He stuck his finger in her pussy and licked it then told her to turn around.

She did and that's when Marvin dropped his drawers and started banging her as she was bent over a chair. After Marvin had bust a nut inside Kelly, he grabbed a duffle bag and they both began counting out a hundred thousand dollars. It took them about forty minutes and Marvin headed out the door on his way to where Cradle was at.

When Marvin pulled up, he saw a Corvette, a BMW, and another fancy car parked on the street. It was clear that these guys were getting money. He called Cradle as soon as he parked and Cradle told him that he was inside and to come in. Marvin walked inside, holding the duffle bag on his shoulder and a pistol in his pants.

"What's up, I'm Cradle."

"Marvin," he said, shaking his hand and fixing his gun inside his pants.

"Just relax, I'm waiting on someone to pull up with the address right now. These my homies Zip and Slaps."

Marvin shook all their hands then sat down. He called Kelly as soon as his butt hit the couch.

"Hello," she answered.

"What's good?" What you doing?" Marvin asked trying to make conversation.

"Nothing, about to get in the shower. What are you doing? Did you make it over there yet?"

"Yeah, I'm over here right now, but the dude with the address hasn't pulled up yet."

"What? What does he mean? Why didn't he say that at first? He coulda just called me when the guy or girl showed up. Let me talk to him because that's a lot of money to just be sitting around with!

She said with an attitude.

"Naw, Naw calm down, just be patient. Everything straight."

"You have your gun?"

"Yeah, you know that."

"How many people over there?"

"Damn Kelly, three."

"Damn what? I'm making sure I know what the hell is going on, this guy can be nuts!"

"I think everything is fine."

"If it was, you wouldn't be on the phone with me."

"Well, bye Kelly, if you're gonna be talking that crazy shit," Marvin said and then he hung up in her face.

She called right back. "Okay I'm sorry, I was just worried about you."

CHAPTER 77

" T hat's fine Kelly. I'll call you back later. I think the guy is walking in right now," he said.

"Ok, call me back."

Mike walked inside by himself and looked around at everyone who was sitting in the living room. "Damn, I ain't know you had a full house."

"It's only four of us and you make five, these are all my guys. Come in the back for a minute."

Cradle said, walking Mike to the back room.

"What sup?" Mike asked.

"Just wanted to make sure everything was straight. I know that's your cousin and all, but he hurt a lot of people's families with his actions," Cradle said.

"I mean, I understand. I don't want to think about that shit, just pay me and I'm out your way. This shit sounds pretty serious to me, especially if you willing to give me ten bricks to know where he's at. So, handle your business," Mike said.

"Ok, so we good then, right?"

"Yeah, fasho."

Cradle walked out first and then they both went into the kitchen where Cradle had the kilos. He was getting ready to give Mike the ten kilos until he felt the steel on the side of his head.

"Don't say a word. If you do I'll blow your fucking brains out," Mike said.

Cradle didn't say a word. He just listened to what Mike said and tried his best to follow his instructions without pissing him off any more than he already was.

"Walk in the living room slowly," Mike told him, as he walked behind him. By the time Mike said a word, Shawna already had everything set up. She had red beams on Marvin and Slaps.

"Everybody put your hands up and don't move. This will be quick. I will be out your way in no time. As you can see, you move the wrong way, you die, simple as that."

Zips was the first one to reach for his gun and Shawna shot him right in the head, killing him instantly.

"I told you don't move. Again, this is not a game. Don't fucking move or you will be next," Mike said calmly, still walking behind Cradle. He knew they all had guns on them, he just had to get them.

Marvin was thinking in his head that this was a set up. He

didn't trust any of them. He didn't know what was going on. All he knew was the guy with the gun was serious and calm.

"Now, what I want ya'll to do is keep your hands up as high as possible in the air. I don't want to kill no one, but I will if you get out of line. Cradle, I'mma let you stand over by them, don't try nothing crazy," Mike said, letting him go. "Now, you have a red dot on your forehead also"

Cradle was looking around, trying to see where the red dot was coming from but he had no clue.

"Ok, now all I'm going to do is pat everyone down just to make sure you all have no guns to shoot me with," he said, going over to Marvin and taking his gun then going over to Slaps and taking two guns off him, "Damn, all serious huh?" he asked and smiled.

He then started to cuff Slaps hands then Marvin was next and Cradle was last. Mike still had three more pair of cuffs because he thought that if would be more people, but instead he just cuffed them all together with two more pair.

CHAPTER 78

"Ok, ya'll can sit down the best way ya'll can."

"Come on man, don't do this shit," Cradle said, finally opening up his mouth.

"Don't do what? I haven't done anything yet," Mike said.

"How much you want?" Marvin added.

"Who the fuck is this lame looking muthafucka?" Mike asked, looking at Cradle.

"Man, his name Marvin. I don't really know him that well."

"Why the fuck you even talking to me Marvin?" Mike said, now catching an attitude. "Now I'm pissed. Why the fuck is this guy talking to me?!" he shouted.

Shawna finally decided to walk in holding two black 45 pistols with beams on them. Plus, she had two ropes, one on her waist line and one on her shoulder. Marvin, Slaps and Cradle had thought there was plenty more people outside that surrounded the house.

"Why didn't you handcuff them in a chair or something?" she asked.

"I don't know. Go get the chairs out the other room and bring them in here," Mike said.

Shawna went and got three chairs and uncuffed them one by one then sat them in each chair and tied their feet up tightly.

Shawna had Marvin, Cradle and Slaps all sitting in a chair, hands cuffed behind them and their feet tied to the chair. She had them lined upside by side as if she was about to teach them in a classroom.

"Ok, I have questions. I can probably put this up right now," he said, putting his gun in the back of his pants. Shawna kept hers pointed.

"Who duffle bag is that over there on the couch? And what's in it?" he asked, as he walked over to the bag and opened it. "Damn! How much is this?"

"Hundred grand, you can have it all, just let me go," Marvin said.

Mike laughed out loud, "Was that a joke?"

"No, it's not a joke," Marvin responded.

"Well, what makes you think I'm not taking this regardless if I let you go or not?" Mike asked.

"I know right?" Shawna was laughing.

"Ok, now Cradle, what makes you think I was gonna just turn on my cousin like that? My blood cousin?" Mike asked.

"Money makes a person do a lot of things you wouldn't normally do. Your momma might kill you over two hundred thousand."

"That's true, but the key word in my question was *I*, Mike pointed out to Cradle. You just thought I was a money hungry ass nigga that would turn on my family huh?"

Cradle didn't say anything. He was feeling too bad inside for even falling for Mike's trick.

"Nothing to say huh? Well ok, tell me where the rest of them bricks are."

"Man, I ran through them things," Cradle said.

"You ran through 70 bricks today?" Mike asked.

"Yeah," Cradle replied.

CHAPTER 79

"Look at the disrespect level right now Shawna. These guys don't respect me at all. First, Marvin told me he will give me money I was already taking, and then Cradle just lied straight to my face. What kind of shit is that Shawna?" Mike asked looking at Shawna.

"Show them what you bout because clearly they don't know," Shawna said, egging me on.

Mike didn't have too many crazy things to play with them how he wanted to. He wanted to torture them all and make them tell everything they knew. Shawna interrupted his thoughts by throwing him a lighter. He took the light and turned the flame up as high as possible and began walking towards Marvin. The flame was about three inches high and Mike put it right in front of Marvin's nose.

Marvin was turning his head from side to side so it was hard for Mike to burn his nose, but Mike was burning each side of his face as he turned it from left to right. He was moving as fast as he could, screaming from the top of his lungs, hoping to stay alive.

After plenty of his skin shriveled, up Marvin finally was able to rock hard enough to tip over in the chair right on his face. "Fuck! What the hell you want man!" Marvin screamed and cried, "I got money I can give you!" he pleaded.

Mike didn't say anything to him. He just smiled and walked over to Cradle with the lighter.

"Come on man. We can seize all this shit right now," Cradle said.

"Tell me where the bricks at and I'll let you live a little longer," Mike promised.

Marvin was still on the floor whining and crying. "Please man, let me go!"

"Man you know Temple not gonna like what you doing right?" Cradle said.

"Oh you still think this is a game. You want to tell me love stories and shit huh? Ok, I got something for you." Mike said, walking over to Cradle and leaning his chair back on the couch, so that his feet were in the air. Mike then began taking off one of his shoes and socks revealing his toes.

CHAPTER 80

"Last chance," Mike said smiling. He was getting a kick out of what he was doing.

"Alright, alright, fuck them bricks. They in the basement inside them duffle bags against the wall. There should be forty there. And fifteen is in the kitchen," Cradle said.

"Cradle, fuck him! You shouldn't tell him shit!" Slaps shouted and spit at Mike at the same time.

Mike wiped the spit off his face, "That was some nasty shit. You a special muthafucka aren't you? I'mma do something special just for you," Mike started pistol whipping him in the face with his gun nonstop. When he finally stopped, Slaps was leaking blood all over the place and his eyes were rolling in the back of his head.

"Get me a knife out that kitchen," Mike said to Shawna. "And bring all the forks you see," he added.

Shawna did just that. There were only four forks, but she bought two big butcher knives also.

Mike grabbed the first fork and jammed it in Slaps face. "Now! How that feel?" Mike shouted.

Slaps tried to spit again, but Mike moved out the way. "Fuck you, muthafucka!" Slaps yelled.

Marvin couldn't see what was going on, but he knew it was painful. He was just hoping Kelly would realize something was wrong due to him not calling her or picking up when she called.

He was waiting on her to call, but she still hadn't called yet.

Mike stuck every fork in Slaps face then he took the knives and butchered Slaps to death, stabbing him more than twenty times all in his chest and stomach area.

Shawna couldn't even watch. There was blood everywhere including on Mike's hands and arms. He had snapped after he seen the sight of blood and it became hard for him to stop.

CHAPTER 81

S oon Marvin's phone was ringing. It was Kelly, but there was no way anyone was going to answer it.

Marvin was happy because he was praying that she'd just show up to see what the problem was.

While Mike was in the bathroom washing his hands, Shawna was watching Marvin and Cradle at gun point.

When Mike was done he went straight in the basement to get the duffle bags filled with drugs.

He brought them outside and loaded the van up. When he came back inside with a baseball bat, Marvin was still on his face and the chair was on top of him because he was still tied to it.

Mike didn't want to shoot them because it would make way too much noise and draw too much attention, so he began beating them with the baseball bat starting with Cradle first. Cradle was only screaming for about five seconds before Mike knocked him unconscious.

Shawna's eyes squinted shut after each hit to Cradle's head. She could hear the cracking of his skull and bones breaking after each hit. There was no way she could watch this neither. She just hated watching it because it turned her stomach.

After Cradle's head was busted wide open and leaking blood, he went over to Marvin, turned him over and did the same thing. Marvin screamed until Mike cracked his jaw right away and ended that. Mike beat him to death as well and when he was done he was so tired and out of breath, Shawna thought he was gonna pass out.

The next morning, JC woke up to Brittany sucking his dick. Ever since he had told her that's what he liked, she did it every single morning no matter what. If she knew he had to get up earlier than usual, he would still get his fix. She never let him leave the house without sucking his dick or giving him some pussy. JC loved that about her. Although she was pregnant, she was still willing to please him.

CHAPTER 82

Today was her birthday and JC had her a surprise that she would love. Both of them had changed their name and moved into a new house that was located in Lima, Ohio.

After JC nutted, he was wide awake and ready to get in the shower to start the day. He had so much planned and he had spent a lot of money planning the day's events for Brittany's birthday.

They both got up and took a shower together then got dressed preparing to first go to breakfast.

"You look so much better without braids. You look like a grown man with your hair cut," Brittany said as she was putting on her panties.

"Thank you. I like it too."

After they dressed and was getting ready to leave out the door, they seen Mike drive up in his black Mercedes. "What he doing over here this early?"

"That's your cousin," Brittany said. She didn't know what to think. She thought JC had something special planned that Mike was a part of as well.

They watched as he got out smiling with a duffle bag in his hand. "Happy Birthday!" he said to Brittany, as he kissed her on the cheek and handed her a wad of money. "Buy you something nice, that's a thousand dollars for you."

"Thank you," she said.

"Yeah, good looking. What up doe? We was on our way to get a bite to eat," JC said.

CHAPTER 83

"Well, let me holla at you before you leave out, it's really important," Mike said.

They walked back in the house, and Brittany went to the room and left JC and Mike in the living room to talk.

"What's up? What's in the bag?" JC asked.

"A gift for you. I hit a lick yesterday for some bricks. This is fifteen inside here. And they all are for you."

"Man, stop playing," JC said smiling.

"I swear J, take a look," Mike said, dropping the bag and unzipping it.

JC looked back at his room door to make sure Brittany was not around. He noticed the room door was opened. "Brittany close the room door for a minute please," He said.

She did just that and JC begins looking through the kilos of cocaine. "Is this real dope?" he asked.

"Yeah man. Look, I took them from your boy Cradle, the nigga who."

"Shh, shh, that's her cousin. Try not to talk that loud."

"Who cousin?"

"Brittany. My baby momma cousin," JC said.

"Man, that nigga wanted to kill you. You trust her?" Mike asked.

"I got her thinking some other shit. Trust me, everything straight. Now you said you took these from Cradle? How the hell you know him?"

"I don't know him like that, but we used to deal with the same people. I've seen him in a few business meetings, that's all. You know my connect Temple use to take us all out to dinner and we would talk about different business ventures."

"So how you manage to get all this?" JC asked.

"Man, you not gonna believe this."

"What?"

"He tried to pay me ten bricks to tell him where you stayed at. I told him ok, and when I got there I fucked over him and two other muthafuckas, one named Marvin and another named Slaps."

"Marvin?"

"Yeah, he was a lame ass nigga I never seen him in my life."

"Well, I hope it's the one I'm thinking about."

"I don't know him, but this is for you."

"This crazy. I don't even believe this," JC said blushing.

"Take 'em. Buy your girl something nice," Mike said.

"Good looking. I appreciate this a lot," JC said, giving him a handshake and a hug.

Mike left and JC couldn't believe Mike gave him fifteen free kilos. At the time, JC was only buying two kilos cash. So to get fifteen free ones, he was overwhelmed. He felt like changing all his plans for the day and doing something even bigger than he had planned. Although he had bought her the new Cadillac coupe, he wanted to take it back and get her something better.

"Brittany! You ready baby?"

"I've been ready. I'm waiting on you. What's in that bag?"

CHAPTER 84

"**W**ork," he replied.

"All of that? Why he give you all of that?"

"This our shit. I'll tell you about it later," he said.

They left their new house driving the car they got last month, the new Buick Lucerne, gray with tinted windows. JC took her to a nice restaurant first and they sat down, ate and talked. JC had fallen in love with her and Brittany was really in love with him as well. JC was loving his new life.

He was working on starting a business and he wanted to launch a women's fragrance line under Brittany's name. Now that Mike had just gave him all those kilos, JC was now able to do whatever he had planned after he cleaned his money up. And that wouldn't be a problem because he had investors calling his phone that bought ounces a week from the people that were selling his dope for him.

Kelly called her mom because she hadn't heard from Marvin. She knew something had to of happened and she knew in her head it was not good.

"Hello dear," her mom answered.

"Mom…I think something happened to Marvin," Kelly said, wanting to cry but he held her tears back because she wasn't sure enough. She was still trying to convince herself that he was okay and to think positive.

"Well honey, when was the last time you spoke to him?"

"Last night, before he left to go meet someone with a lot of money."

"Do you know who he went to meet?"

CHAPTER 85

"Yes, the owner of Merido's old store. I went up there and the person that was working there said they hadn't heard from Cradle yet. I called Cradle also and he didn't answer. The phone didn't even ring. Marvin's phone's isn't ringing either. I don't know what's going on."

"Well just relax right now. Do you know where Marvin was going to meet whoever he was meeting?"

"I had it wrote down, but I gave the paper to Marvin. I tried to call Merido, but he's not answering. I'm sure he knows where Cradle lives."

"Cradle?"

"Yeah mom, that's who he went to meet."

"Well, do you think Cradle has something to do with it?"

"I don't know. Right now, I just want to find Marvin. Can I speak to Merido please?" Kelly asked.

Merido got right on the phone. "What's going on?" he asked.

"Marvin hasn't called since last night. Something happened when he was at Cradle's house last night, I know it," she said.

"Wait, wait, calm down. He went to meet Cradle?"

"Yeah and he never called me afterwards."

"Ok, let me do some tracking to find Cradle and I'll give you a call back as soon as I hear something."

"Well, I'm on my way over there."

"Over where?" Merido asked.

"To your house. Me and the kids."

"Oh, ok come on."

"Ok, bye," Kelly said, hanging up. She felt a lot better now. She knew Merido was going to find out what happened. Kelly packed her and the kids up and left in a hurry. She was scared because she had no idea if someone was after her now. She knew JC was still out there, but there was nothing in her mind thinking he had anything to do with this one.

An hour later, she arrived at her mom's house and went inside with her kids. The kids ran straight to their grandma hugging and kissing her while Kelly went in the other room to talk to Merido. He had a sad look on his face and Kelly knew something had happened.

"What? He's dead isn't he?" she said, just feeling it inside her.

Merido didn't talk, he just added his head yes and Kelly broke down and cried her heart out for hours as Merido held her tightly in his arms. Kelly was regretting everything's she had ever done bad to people. She felt like this was karma. But this karma was horrible. The worst she had ever experienced. She had no clue how she would tell her kids about their daddy. She had no idea what she would do without him. How she would go through a whole day without seeing his face. She was crushed and she could feel nothing inside besides pain.

CHAPTER 86

After hearing the story, Merido wanted revenge. He promised himself, if JC had anything to do with this or any ties he was calling up the mafia he used to run with back in the day. They were very dangerous, and they were able to track anybody down, no matter what.

Later that day, it was said that the police had phone records with one lead. That made Merido call his buddy that was part of the force to let him hear the phone records. They met up and Merido got in the black van with him.

"How are you?" Merido asked, shaking his hand.

"I'm good. We have to make this fast. This is the phone company Mr. Mike Cakes goes through. He's the owner of a multimillion dollar company. The Feds have been investigating this guy for years now. He escaped a big indictment years ago and changed his last name to Cakes."

"Why he do that?"

"He's wanted for 56 murders. This guy is dangerous. I mean he's the real deal. After I seen the report and what he did to the four victims in that house, I knew it was some of his work. This fucker is sick."

"So where can I find him?"

"Oh, he's the cousin of the young guy that made America's Most Wanted, Jason Cakes."

"Sure is!" Merido smiled. "Ain't this a bitch?" he said with an accent.

"Yeah, but we gonna get to the bottom of this and nail them both. We believe JC had taken his place for a while. I personally think they working together."

Merido knew that he had no idea what he was talking about. Merido was shocked that he knew more than the police. "Where can I find him?"

"Ohio. He lives with his wife in a huge house."

"Write it down for me," Merido said, cutting him off.

As soon as Merido got out of the van, he called a number he thought he would never use again. He was a serious player for someone like JC. He needed someone who didn't mind getting his hands dirty.

CHAPTER 87

The next day after getting his morning head from Brittany, JC laid back and thought of how good his life had turned out to be. He had the girl by his side that was down for him, a baby on the way, a boy at that, and his money was straight, thanks to Mike.

Mike was cut from a different cloth, a real solid brother. JC looked over at the bathroom where Brittany had just taken a bath and now her foot was on the edge of the tub shaving her legs. She looked his way and smiled.

JC reached over and grabbed his cell phone to call Mike, but his voicemail was full. He was supposed to call JC this morning. JC wanted to go hang with him, let him know how much he appreciates the love Mike has shown him. JC got dressed and went into the bathroom where Brittany was shaving her pussy, just the way he liked it, no interference when his tongue went to work. "I'mma head to Mike's and see what's up, maybe go hang out or a few. Why don't you go shopping for some baby stuff, get us a crib, car seat, start looking at some lil' Jordan's for my lil' man," JC suggested, holding her from behind. His dick starting to get hard again.

"I think I'm just gonna chill first. That morning sickness hit me kind of hard, or maybe it was that big dick of yours gagging me," she teased smiling at him in the mirror.

"You want me to pick up something from the pharmacy?" he asked kind of concerned.

"Nah, I'm straight baby. I just need to relax. Have fun and tell Mike I said hi."

JC kissed her goodbye, patted her belly, and made sure he left her a few thousand on the dresser in case she changed her mind about shopping. He drove over to Mike's house and saw a black Benz with tinted windows in the driveway. JC got out and knocked on the door. When no one answered, he looked in the window and didn't see anyone. He hoped none of the neighbors thought he was a burglar and called the cops, that would be messed up. JC walked off the porch and headed for his car when he saw something leaking from the bottom of Mike's Benz. Concerned it was something that might cause a break down, JC bent over and dabbed the reddish liquid with is finger and smelled the substance. It wasn't hydraulic fluid and he couldn't figure out just what it was. Then he walked to the passenger side and saw it wasn't coming from under the car like he thought. It was coming from inside the car and flowing downhill to the driver's door. JC opened the door praying the alarm wasn't set and saw Mike's head sitting in the driver's seat without the body attached. He had to stop himself from gagging at the smell. Flies flew from Mike's mouth, annoyed at the intrusion. Out of the corner of his eye, JC saw something in the backseat. It was Mike's wife and kids, also beheaded and propped up in a pyramid formation.

From the look of the wounds, it appeared their heads were cut off with something jagged, judging from the uneven cuts on the flesh that hung from the heads. The kids' eyes had also been gouged out, with money rolled inside. Mike's eyes had been open, whoever did this probably made him watch. JC closed his car quickly and sped off, looking in the rearview mirror the whole time. Worried he might be followed, he took an alley.

CHAPTER 88

By the time JC got home, he found the door kicked in. He walked in carefully and saw the place torn up like someone was searching for something. He peeked into the bedroom, whispering Brittany's name. No answer, and he found blood on the bed and one of her shoes in the hallway where she probably struggled. JC went to the basement and saw the ceiling panels had been taken off and all the dope was gone. They never thought to look in the furnace duct work where he kept some money. JC put the money in a gym bag, pocketed two extra clips for his pistol and left the house. As soon as he started up the engine his phone rang, Brittany's number flashed on the display. Relieved he asked, "Baby, where you at?"

There was silence for a second and then a familiar sounding voice said, "Baby, with me!"

"Who this and where's Brittany?" JC asked the woman on the other end.

"If you want to see her alive you better come get her. Her life for yours JC," Kelly told him, hoping he would take the bait. But in her heart she knew JC was too selfish. His self-survival instincts would never allow him to sacrifice his life for another.

"Let me talk to her and hear that she's alive. How do I know you didn't already kill her?"

There was a pause and then he heard Brittany's voice, "I'm sorry JC. They snuck up on me when I was lying down. Don't worry about me, just run. They'll kill us both anyway, just leave!!!" she cried out, as her sentence ended with a scream.

"That was her finger we cut off. Imagine our surprise when I found out she was pregnant with your baby. Congratulations, JC. That is so sweet, the perfect family. The clock is ticking JC. Meet me at the abandoned Farmer Jack's warehouse by the airport, you have an hour."

"I love you JC! Gooo!!!" Brittany yelled in the background as his phone started beeping indicating a low battery then it died. Enraged, JC threw the phone out the window and headed towards the freeway. He loved Brittany, but they would kill them both, and he knew it. She told him to choose his life over hers. Tears ran down his cheeks as he headed south, wanting to put as much distance between him and those who would kill him. When he got tired he pulled over and slept, gun always in his hand. When he got past Tennessee, he took a nap at a rest area. In the morning when he woke up, he was surprised to find out his engine wouldn't turn over. He opened the hood, but couldn't figure out what was wrong. He went into the rest area center and saw a number for a local towing service and called them. The man who answered promised to be there within the hour.

CHAPTER 89

While he was waiting, he bought a cup of coffee and a pack of donuts, and sat at the picnic table. JC whistled loudly when he saw a silver Bentley pull up. A woman got out wearing a black skirt that had a slit along one side, with a sheer white blouse on and white bra underneath. The red heels she wore were about three inches high, and she had a nice set of titties bouncing as she walked by and a round little booty.

"Excuse me, you are drop dead gorgeous," JC said as she passed him.

The woman had a complexion that was a couple shades darker than caramel, and she smelled nice. She just smiled at JC ignoring his greeting and walked inside.

A few minutes later, she came back out, and bought a Pepsi and a snickers.

"So you just gonna ignore a compliment, huh?"

"Sorry, I had other things on my mind. How are you doing?" she asked being nice. "And thank you."

"I'm ok now that you spoke back. Where you from? I hear a lil' accent."

She blushed, checking him out from head to toe, quickly noticing his dick print through his jeans. "I'm from Atlanta, Georgia. How about you?"

"I'm from Michigan. You going back home? I'm going with you. You bouta be my new wife."

She sat down, giggling trying to drink her pop, taking a break from the driving. "Whatever! Yeah, I had to drop off a few things in New York, and I hate planes. Where you going? Your wife? Oh really?" she asked smiling.

"Nowhere special, I'm just doing me. Seeing where the road takes me. My car messed up and the tow truck won't be here for an hour."

"That sucks, sorry about that," she stated standing up and started to walk away when JC stopped her.

"What's your name, baby?"

"Gloria, why?"

"I'm JC, just in case I see you again."

Gloria smiled at him and said, "Here, take my business card. Maybe you'll feel the pull of Atlanta calling to you."

JC put the car in his pocket, "I will def be using this real soon," he said, smiling.

Gloria blushed and took a long drink of her pop, then licked her lips. "I'll buy you breakfast when you come to town at one of my places. Good luck with your car, bye," Gloria said, walking away towards her car.

She turned around and glanced back to see if he was looking at her, pretending there was something on her heel, "Call me if you need my help, I will gladly take you with me," she said blowing a kiss his way.

CHAPTER 90

F inally, the tow truck arrived two hours later. The old guy running the truck slid JC's BMW onto the flat bed. He had on stained overalls, with 'Bubba's Fix-It Station' written on the back.

Can I catch a ride with you into town?" JC asked the old guy, who was busy stuffing chewing tobacco into his mouth.

"Makes me no difference," he said as tobacco dripped out of his mouth and onto his filthy beard.

"So where we headed, school?"

"Labanon, Tennessee. There's a school there for the youngins."

"Nah, I didn't mean that kind of school," JC began to explain, but then stopped, not even trying to bridge the generation gap. "Is there a hotel or something I can stay at while you figure out what's wrong with my car?"

"We got the Possum Creek Motel in town and then there's

Widow Carter's place. She usually has a room or two to rent in her house, but I hear her dogs got fleas and such. Plus, she don't take kindly to coloreds!"

"She don't like colored what?"

"Colored people, boy! She don't like your kind!" he said, spitting out the window.

JC was about to shoot this KKK loving fool until he saw the town come into view. "Just drop me at the motel," he said, as the truck passed a Barney Fife looking cop sitting in front of a store.

The tow truck stopped in front of a dark green garage with peeling paint and warped overhead doors. The old guy got out paying JC no mind and walked into the office with JC following behind, "Hey, you can't be leaving my ride out there for someone to steal, that's a $65,000.00 car," he didn't want to mention the bag of money he had in the trunk.

The old man sat down and pulled out a mason jar full of some clear liquid and took a swig. "Ain't no one gonna steal that jar! It ain't got no gun rack, no winch, and no 4 x 4," he laughed at the idea of someone wanting to take JC's car.

"Look across the street. I don't know why you gettin' a room and such, the car be ready in a couple of hours. That'll be $250.00."

"$250.00 for what? You haven't even done anything yet."

"I done towed your car and it's either the battery or alternator, sonny!"

JC peeled off three hundred and walked outside, squinting

against the sun. He moved across the street and saw the motel sign laying on the ground. A sign which promised free cable and air conditioning, not to mention half off dinners at 'Granny's Kitchen'. JC walked into the office of the twelve room motel and rang the cowbell on the desk next to the sign that read, 'Ring for Service'.

CHAPTER 91

A few minutes later, JC heard a girl's voice yell from the back, "Hold your horses, I'm coming!" A dark haired white girl, skinny as a rail came out, wearing a blue sundress with yellow daisies printed on it. JC saw she had a sprinkle of freckles on her nose, and he guessed she was nineteen or twenty. "Hi, welcome to Possum Creek Motel, I'm Sally Ann!" Sally Ann was about as country as the CMT videos JC had seen in prison. Her hair hung down in two pig tails, with no shoes on her feet, and friendly as hell.

"Hi, I'm JC. I need me a room for the night, my car broke down," he said, motioning his hand towards the garage behind him where his black BMW car still sat on the flatbed truck.

"Oh, yeah. I seen one of them on TV before. Is that one of those foreign cars? It's a real pretty color. Will you be staying alone or do you have a guest?"

"Hmmm, alone and thanks. What do ya'll do for fun down

here?" JC asked, signing the paper with an alias. She didn't even ask for ID

"Well, we go down to Cooper's Pond and fish, on some nights Johnny Ray plays a mean fiddle out back, but usually me and my cousin, Sarah, we just drink some moonshine and gossip about what's going on."

"You drink moonshine? For real?" JC asked, thinking she was fucking with him.

"Everyone drinks moonshine in Labanon! You ever drink any?"

JC shook his head and asked, "Ya'll smoke some tree?"

"Tree? What's that? Why would we smoke a tree?"

JC lowered his voice and said, "You know, some weed? Marijuana?"

"Oh, yeah. But the stuff the boys around here grow ain't that great and gives me a headache. Sometimes we go to Memphis and get some from Sarah's cousin. Why? You got some?"

JC nodded and said, "Hey, I got an idea. Why don't you and your girl come to my room when you get off work and bring some of that moonshine? We'll have ourselves a little party."

Sally Ann bit at her fingernail with blue polish on it and then smiled, "Okay, take room twelve then. It has a queen sized bed and a big shower. Plus, it's at the end. But we gotta be quiet, I ain't supposed to fraternize with the guests. And I'm supposed to charge you an extra ten dollars for that room, but I'll let it slide," she added while passing him a brass key with the number twelve on it.

They touched hands as the key passed between them and JC

made sure his finger lingered on hers for a few extra seconds. Sally Ann blushed making her freckles look like stars in the sky.

"I can't wait to see you tonight. I think we gonna have fun," JC said, as he walked out the door leaving the girl's heart beating fast.

JC's room had an old door and he could smell the mustiness from the not so clean carpet that had water damage stains on it. The antique A/C unit hummed violently against the rusty brackets that held it in the window and the TV was a big bubble RCA that had to be from the 90's along with an old style cable box. He took a quick shower and laid down for a nap, keeping his gun close as he heard some critters out back making weird noises. An hour later, he was awakened by the sounds of gunfire in the distance.

CHAPTER 92

After washing his face, he walked outside and went to the vending machine he passed by earlier in between his room and the office. He pulled out some dollar bills and bought a Pepsi, a pack of Twinkies, and a Pay Day to munch on. He didn't want to go into town and risk a confrontation with these hillbillies. He looked across the street and saw his car was off the flatbed and inside the garage, where the old dude was under the hood wrenching on something. JC was going to leave when it was fixed, but he needed a break from driving for the night. Plus, the two girls were coming over to hang out.

A few hours later, there was a knock at the door. When he opened it, he saw Sally Ann wearing a pair of cut off shorts, and a halter top that showed her perky tits. Behind her came a shyer, slightly uglier version of Sally Ann.

"You must be Sarah. Come on in," JC invited them. Sarah was shorter than Sally Ann and plumper. Her hair was what some might call dishwater blonde, with bucked teeth, and big ass ears, like Dumbo sized.

Sally Ann had a gallon jug of some clear stuff, probably used to be a milk container. And Sarah had a bag filled with something in it. "What's in the bag, Sarah?" JC asked.

"Oh, Sally Ann said you hadn't been to town so I thought you might be hungry."

"I'm starving, thanks. What you got for me?" JC asked opening the bag.

"There's some venison, chicken gizzards and a pie Aunt Mable made last night."

JC tried the venison and that wasn't so bad, but he stayed away from the gizzards, saving the pie for later. "Here let me roll you something up and get this party started," he declared as he pulled out a sack of some premium buds. He rolled a fat joint in a matter of seconds and lit it up, passing it to Sally first then he got to rolling another.

"This is good JC," Sally claimed, coughing on her first hit as did Sarah. She opened the jug and took a swig before handing it to JC.

JC took a good swallow and spit it all over the back wall, "God damn, what the hell is that? Gasoline? Ya'll trying to kill me?" he asked, still coughing.

CHAPTER 93

They both giggled and Sarah took the jug and had a swallow, "Ain't nothing wrong with that. That's pappy's best bottle. Try smaller sips, you ain't used to nothing like this. This is equal to 150 proof or better," she stated proudly as if a blue ribbon was being awarded. Sarah sat cross-legged on the bed and JC could make out her pussy hairs coming from the side of her underwear with the yellow dress she had on.

"So what was all the shooting and hollering I heard earlier?" JC asked, taking smaller drinks. The booze still burned on the way down.

"Oh, that was them recreating the Civil War battle when we sent these Yanks clear back into Kentucky. There's always some celebrating about the war going on," Sally Ann boasted proudly.

By the time they finished both joints and drank about a pint of moonshine, JC had snuggled up against Sally and began kissing her neck. He was surprised by how quickly she kissed him back and started grabbing at his dick hidden beneath his jeans. Sarah just sat to the side watching them for a second then she used the remote and turned on the TV to the porn station. Soon moans could be heard from the TV and from them. Sarah started playing with her own pussy while Sally pulled down JC's pants and started licking on his dick, not being able to suck more than a few inches of it at a time. Sarah came from behind and pulled Sally's shorts off and started fingering her wet pussy. JC pulled Sarah's dress off and started playing with her big tits. He pulled out of Sally's mouth and moved behind where Sarah was and stuck his dick into her tight pussy, moving slowly an inch at a time until half his dick was inside her. She fell into Sally who opened her legs for Sarah to lick on until they both started to cum and yell like wild animals. JC pulled out and shot his wad all over Sarah's back. Then Sally got on top of JC's dick and pushed it in as far as she could then she started riding him. Sarah drank more moonshine. He let Sally have her fun then he turned her over and rammed his fat dick all the way in until she moaned loudly while Sarah plopped her fat pussy in Sally's face, letting her moan and lick her into an orgasm. By the time JC came again, both girls had cum three times. Then he sat back and let them lick and suck on his dick until he came again. JC was thinking about fucking them in the ass when he heard a voice outside yelling.

"Sally Ann? Sally Ann? I know you around there!"

"Who is that?" JC asked, getting up and heading for his gun underneath the mattress.

"That's Tommy, he used to date Sally Ann, and was supposed to marry her, but Sally broke it off on the account that he's got a small penis!" Sarah said, making her and Sally laugh. The weed made them silly as hell.

Tommy heard them laughing while he stood outside the door, "Sally Ann you better bring your ass outta there before I tell your daughter," he waited a few seconds more and kicked the door in.

Both the girls squealed in surprise and Tommy turned out to be a corn Fed boy of about eighteen weighing at least three hundred pounds and was so tall he had to stoop to come into the room, followed by two other boys. One had a baseball bat in his hand, wearing a pair of overalls and no shirt underneath. He had reddish hair, and a ruddy complexion. Next to enter was a dark haired boy, a little older with a bushy beard wearing a pair of jeans with holes in them and a t-shirt a size or two too small. He was short but barrel chested and held a rusty Bowie knife in his hand.

CHAPTER 94

" Sally Ann what are doing with this, nigger?" Tommy asked putting a sheet over her nakedness. "I ain't gonna marry you now, ain't no boy gonna marry you after being with his kind!"

"You boys better get out of my room!" JC told them, holding his pistol to the side.

He could see in their eyes that they weren't used to taking orders from a black man and had no intention of leaving without leaving their mark on him. The red haired boy with the bat moved towards JC and raised his weapon as he approached. JC squeezed the trigger and two bullets entered his chest. The next round caught the dark haired one in the shoulder, the second in his jaw before he fell to the carpet. The girls screamed. JC walked up to Tommy who had no weapon and stuck the gun into his forehead and pulled the trigger once, spraying his brain matter all over Sarah's yellow dress.

JC quickly dressed and grabbed all of his things and sprinted across the street to the garage that was now empty with the lights off. The office door was locked, but he pulled on the overhead doors and they opened with a loud creak waking not only the dead, but two pit bulls that lunged at him. The first one knocked JC down as the other lunged at his neck slashing at his eyes with his sharp nails.

He pushed the 80 pound dog off of him as the other one circled him like prey. JC reached into his pocket and pulled out the gun, that probably only had two or three bullets left and fired one at the circling dog hitting it in the leg, but he still had fight in him. The other sensing the danger leaped at JC from behind biting his shirt before JC shot him in the head. It took a few seconds before the jaw stopped chomping on him as the brain received the message that it was dead. The smaller and quicker dog tried to dodge the bullet as it caught him in the chest, mid-flight as he jumped at JC's face, then the gun clicked on empty. With no choice, JC punched the dog in the face and ran into the garage and got into his car, which thankfully started on the first try. He backed out, running over the pit, crushing his head like a pumpkin.

CHAPTER 95

JC could hear shouts in the distance and gunshots going off not far from where he was. It was time to get going before they lynched his ass. JC stomped on the gas and took off the way he came in, then found the freeway by luck. He sped off into the night, hoping they didn't chase after him. It wasn't until he passed the state line and entered Mississippi that he breathed a sigh of relief.

When JC stopped for gas, the sun was rising in the east, ushering in a new day. He looked over in the bathroom and noticed a few scratches on his face from where the dog's paw had swiped at him. His shirt was torn beyond repair in the back, and his jeans were dirty. He must have looked like a homeless guy who stole a BMW to the clerk at the counter when he came in. JC walked out into the store and bought a white t-shirt and gray sweats featuring the Mississippi Bulldogs mascot. He bought a bottle of some off brand orange juice and a breakfast sandwich that looked processed and filled up the gas tank. When JC was done he got into the car and his car failed to start. Not believing it, he turned the ignition over again and got nothing, no power whatsoever. He popped the hood and looked inside and saw a wire going from the battery to the alternator. The old guy had rigged his car just to make it far enough so that he wouldn't come back to complain. JC slammed the hood down and got a dirty look from the cashier who was watching him. He reached into his pocket and felt the business card Gloria had given him. He needed to get out of there as soon as possible. He grabbed some change out of the car and went to the payphone on the wall of the station, praying Gloria picked up.

"Hello?" a woman's voiced asked on the other end.

"Gloria, thank God you picked up. I'mma need a ride into Atlanta if you're up for it," JC said hoping she wouldn't say no.

There was a few seconds of silence where JC thought she had hung up, "Who is this?"

"Oh, right, sorry, this JC. The guy you met at the rest area in Tennessee."

"Oh, hi. Now what do you want me to do?"

"My car broke down in Mississippi and I need to get going now. I don't want to be waiting around while they fuck me over again. It broke down earlier and they did some screwed up job, but now the car went out again. I was thinking maybe Atlanta was the place to be since that's where you at."

"JC, I don't even know you. I meant I'd see you like in a social setting."

"You might be a serial rapist chasing down men for all I know," JC pointed out.

"When was the last time you heard of a woman being a serial rapist?"

"I'm just saying! Look, I can pay you for your trouble, that's not a problem. I will give you anything you want, with interest."

CHAPTER 96

"Anything I want?" she said in a sexy voice while running her tongue over her cherry lips gloss. "Where are you in Mississippi?" she asked wondering how far back she was going to have to go.

"Hang on," JC said as he ran inside and asked the clerk. Once he told her, she agreed and told him it would take a couple of hours to swing back his way. As luck would have it, she stayed the night not too far from him at a hotel and had just gotten back on the road.

"This is going to cost you big time, Mr. JC."

"Hey, I got you. Dinner is on me."

"If you think I'm coming back for dinner, you crazy boy. You better be supplying the dessert too."

JC laughed and said, "You ain't gonna be disappointed."

He hung up and waited in his car, until the heat started getting to him in the air-condition less car, then he went inside and paid the guy fifty bucks to let him stay inside for a while. Two and a half hours later he saw Gloria's Bentley pull in. He grabbed his bag of money and threw it in the trunk when she opened it from inside then he climbed into the working A/C.

"Thanks a lot Gloria, I really appreciate it." He placed a thousand dollars into her hand.

"You don't have to give me money JC. That ain't what I need?"

"I want to, please. You really helping me out. And I got you on whatever else you need me for," he said to her. Though in his head he was thinking, she had no idea how much she was helping him out. "I will call my cousin to pick my car up later, he has a tow truck," JC lied.

"It will take you some time to get used to the heat," she told him as she drove out of the gas station and headed back towards Atlanta. "So what you gonna do in Atlanta?"

"I'm not sure, I'mma just hang there for a while see what's what."

"Well, it's got a good economy. I'm not sure what kind of work you do, but you shouldn't have a problem finding a job."

"I'm straight with money right now, I think I'mma just chill, see the sights. You gonna be my tour guide?" JC asked running his hand down her arm.

She felt the goose bumps pop up on her arms making her shiver from his caress. "Oh, you think you a playa', huh?"

CHAPTER 97

"I ain't no playa', I just like you and I think you like me too, otherwise you wouldn't have picked me up, right?"

"Maybe, we'll see. I just met you and all."

"I just met you and I like what I see. I'm single and you single, so let's see what's up!"

"You are a smooth talker, JC. I'll give you that. So where you gonna stay at when you get in Atlanta?"

"I'm not sure, I haven't even thought that far ahead. I guess a hotel or something. Is there one near you?"

"Not really, I live in a gated community outside Atlanta. There's plenty of hotels downtown though."

"I guess, I'll have to stay at one of them, unless you want me to stay with you?" JC asked, looking out the window casually.

"You are crazy boy. Like I'm just gonna let you into where I sleep," she said thinking he was crazy and maybe she shouldn't have picked him up.

"Look, I'mma be honest with you Gloria because I like you. I got money and want to start my life over in a difference city, with different people. Michigan is so messed up, I don't even feel like it's my home anymore, ya feel me? Maybe I'm coming on too strong, but honestly, you are someone I will put my all into. I will actually move to Atlanta for good with you."

Gloria's heart was beating pretty fast as he talked to her, and she had to admit she liked him. It had been a minute since she met a decent guy, someone who wasn't playing her for the money or looking for another mother to cuddle them. "I don't know JC. I do like you, you sexy as hell, and you in shape, and you called me when you needed help, most guys wouldn't do that. I know what you mean about your home not feeling like a home anymore I been in a couple bad relationships where I felt like that. Maybe you do need a fresh start."

"I do for sure. Let's just see what happens."

"I'm gonna do this, I have a room over my garage. Probably meant to be a driver's quarters or something, but it's fully furnished, it has its own bathroom, and a kitchen. You can stay in there and we'll go hang out and see how we get along, okay? That way we get to know each other and that way I can find out if you are a serial killer."

"I'mma take that, just because I'm going to show you what a real man be like. How long we got until we get to your place?" JC asked yawning and leaning the seat back.

"We got about three and half hours still, go ahead and take a nap. I'll wake you when we get there. You gonna need your energy, you best believe that," Gloria said, looking over at him as he closed his eyes.

"We'll see about that baby," JC told her, as he let the sounds of the road put him to sleep.

Gloria put her phone on vibrate so she didn't wake him if someone called. He did look tired, but she'd get him squared away and looking good. They drove like that for the rest of the trip, she kept looking over and JC wondering who he was and what kind of story he had to tell. She had to figure him out, but until then she was gonna use his body to the fullest.

JC found it hard to fall asleep, he was headed into an unknown world down in Atlanta, and he didn't know the rules or the players. He felt along the side of the passenger door and made sure his gun hadn't fallen under the seat in case the cops stopped them. There was no way he was headed to jail. He looked up a couple of times and saw the signs showing Georgia was close, promising beautiful views and unnamed adventures. He had enough adventures to last anyone a lifetime, he really did need to just chill for a while. He soon nodded into a deep sleep.

By the time they arrived to Gloria's house, a simmering fog had fallen over the Atlanta area, giving the town an eerie look. They entered the rural area, with grand mansions, big condos, and elite neighborhoods. She then punched in the entry code to gain access. JC looked up trying to get his bearings, and reached for his pistol, when he seen Kelly and Merido standing in the way of the gate holding guns......

Lock Down Publications and Ca$h Presents assisted publishing
packages.

BASIC PACKAGE $499
Editing
Cover Design
Formatting

UPGRADED PACKAGE $800
Typing
Editing
Cover Design
Formatting

ADVANCE PACKAGE $1,200
Typing
Editing
Cover Design
Formatting
Copyright registration
Proofreading
Upload book to Amazon

LDP SUPREME PACKAGE $1,500
Typing
Editing
Cover Design
Formatting
Copyright registration
Proofreading
Set up Amazon account
Upload book to Amazon
Advertise on LDP Amazon and Facebook page

***Other services available upon request. Additional charges may apply
Lock Down Publications
P.O. Box 944
Stockbridge, GA 30281-9998
Phone # 470 303-9761

Submission Guideline

Submit the first three chapters of your completed manuscript to ldpsubmissions@gmail.com, subject line: Your book's title. The manuscript must be in a .doc file and sent as an attachment. Document should be in Times New Roman, double spaced and in size 12 font. Also, provide your synopsis and full contact information. If sending multiple submissions, they must each be in a separate email.

Have a story but no way to send it electronically? You can still submit to LDP/Ca$h Presents. Send in the first three chapters, written or typed, of your completed manuscript to:

LDP: Submissions Dept
Po Box 944
Stockbridge, Ga 30281

DO NOT send original manuscript. Must be a duplicate.

Provide your synopsis and a cover letter containing your full contact information.

Thanks for considering LDP and Ca$h Presents.

NEW RELEASES

BORN IN THE GRAVE 3 by SELF MADE TAY

PROTÉGÉ OF A LEGEND 3 by COREY ROBINSON

GORILLAZ IN THE TRENCHES 2 by SAYNOMORE

BLOOD OF A GOON by ROMELL TUKES

THE COCAINE PRINCESS 8 by KING RIO

3X KRAZY III

STRAIGHT BEAST MODE III

De'Kari

KINGPIN KILLAZ IV

STREET KINGS III

PAID IN BLOOD III

CARTEL KILLAZ IV

DOPE GODS III

Hood Rich

SINS OF A HUSTLA II

ASAD

YAYO V

Bred In The Game 2

S. Allen

THE STREETS WILL TALK II

By Yolanda Moore

SON OF A DOPE FIEND III

HEAVEN GOT A GHETTO III

SKI MASK MONEY III

By Renta

LOYALTY AIN'T PROMISED III

By Keith Williams

I'M NOTHING WITHOUT HIS LOVE II

SINS OF A THUG II

TO THE THUG I LOVED BEFORE II

IN A HUSTLER I TRUST II

By Monet Dragun

QUIET MONEY IV

EXTENDED CLIP III

THUG LIFE IV

By **Trai'Quan**

THE STREETS MADE ME IV

By **Larry D. Wright**

IF YOU CROSS ME ONCE III

ANGEL V

By **Anthony Fields**

THE STREETS WILL NEVER CLOSE IV

By **K'ajji**

HARD AND RUTHLESS III

KILLA KOUNTY IV

By **Khufu**

MONEY GAME III

By **Smoove Dolla**

JACK BOYS VS DOPE BOYS IV

A GANGSTA'S QUR'AN V

COKE GIRLZ II

COKE BOYS II

LIFE OF A SAVAGE V

CHI'RAQ GANGSTAS V

SOSA GANG III

BRONX SAVAGES II

BODYMORE KINGPINS II

BLOOD OF A GOON II

By **Romell Tukes**

MURDA WAS THE CASE III

Elijah R. Freeman

AN UNFORESEEN LOVE IV

BABY, I'M WINTERTIME COLD III

By **Meesha**

QUEEN OF THE ZOO III
By **Black Migo**
CONFESSIONS OF A JACKBOY III
By **Nicholas Lock**
KING KILLA II
By **Vincent "Vitto" Holloway**
BETRAYAL OF A THUG III
By **Fre$h**
THE MURDER QUEENS III
By **Michael Gallon**
THE BIRTH OF A GANGSTER III
By **Delmont Player**
TREAL LOVE II
By **Le'Monica Jackson**
FOR THE LOVE OF BLOOD III
By **Jamel Mitchell**
RAN OFF ON DA PLUG II
By **Paper Boi Rari**
HOOD CONSIGLIERE III
By **Keese**
PRETTY GIRLS DO NASTY THINGS II
By **Nicole Goosby**
LOVE IN THE TRENCHES II
By **Corey Robinson**
IT'S JUST ME AND YOU II
By **Ah'Million**
FOREVER GANGSTA III

By Adrian Dulan

GORILLAZ IN THE TRENCHES III

By SayNoMore

THE COCAINE PRINCESS IX

By King Rio

CRIME BOSS II

Playa Ray

LOYALTY IS EVERYTHING III

Molotti

HERE TODAY GONE TOMORROW II

By Fly Rock

REAL G'S MOVE IN SILENCE II

By Von Diesel

GRIMEY WAYS IV

By Ray Vinci

Available Now

RESTRAINING ORDER **I & II**

By **CA$H & Coffee**

LOVE KNOWS NO BOUNDARIES **I II & III**

By **Coffee**

RAISED AS A GOON I, II, III & IV

BRED BY THE SLUMS I, II, III

BLAST FOR ME I & II

ROTTEN TO THE CORE I II III

A BRONX TALE I, II, III

DUFFLE BAG CARTEL I II III IV V VI

HEARTLESS GOON I II III IV V

A SAVAGE DOPEBOY I II

DRUG LORDS I II III

CUTTHROAT MAFIA I II

KING OF THE TRENCHES

By **Ghost**

LAY IT DOWN **I & II**

LAST OF A DYING BREED I II

BLOOD STAINS OF A SHOTTA I & II III

By **Jamaica**

LOYAL TO THE GAME I II III

LIFE OF SIN I, II III

By **TJ & Jelissa**

BLOODY COMMAS I & II

SKI MASK CARTEL I II & III

KING OF NEW YORK I II,III IV V

RISE TO POWER I II III

COKE KINGS I II III IV V

BORN HEARTLESS I II III IV

KING OF THE TRAP I II

By **T.J. Edwards**

IF LOVING HIM IS WRONG…I & II

LOVE ME EVEN WHEN IT HURTS I II III

By **Jelissa**

WHEN THE STREETS CLAP BACK I & II III

THE HEART OF A SAVAGE I II III IV

MONEY MAFIA I II

LOYAL TO THE SOIL I II III

By **Jibril Williams**

A DISTINGUISHED THUG STOLE MY HEART I II & III

LOVE SHOULDN'T HURT I II III IV

RENEGADE BOYS I II III IV

PAID IN KARMA I II III

SAVAGE STORMS I II III

AN UNFORESEEN LOVE I II III

BABY, I'M WINTERTIME COLD I II

By **Meesha**

A GANGSTER'S CODE I &, II III

A GANGSTER'S SYN I II III

THE SAVAGE LIFE I II III

CHAINED TO THE STREETS I II III

BLOOD ON THE MONEY I II III

A GANGSTA'S PAIN I II III

By J-Blunt

PUSH IT TO THE LIMIT

By **Bre' Hayes**

BLOOD OF A BOSS **I, II, III, IV, V**

SHADOWS OF THE GAME

TRAP BASTARD

By **Askari**

THE STREETS BLEED MURDER **I, II & III**

THE HEART OF A GANGSTA I II& III

By **Jerry Jackson**

CUM FOR ME I II III IV V VI VII VIII

An **LDP Erotica Collaboration**

BRIDE OF A HUSTLA **I II & II**

THE FETTI GIRLS **I, II& III**

CORRUPTED BY A GANGSTA I, II III, IV

BLINDED BY HIS LOVE

THE PRICE YOU PAY FOR LOVE I, II ,III

DOPE GIRL MAGIC I II III

By **Destiny Skai**

WHEN A GOOD GIRL GOES BAD

By **Adrienne**

THE COST OF LOYALTY I II III

By Kweli

A GANGSTER'S REVENGE **I II III & IV**

THE BOSS MAN'S DAUGHTERS I II III IV V

A SAVAGE LOVE **I & II**

BAE BELONGS TO ME I II

A HUSTLER'S DECEIT I, II, III

WHAT BAD BITCHES DO I, II, III

SOUL OF A MONSTER I II III

KILL ZONE

A DOPE BOY'S QUEEN I II III

TIL DEATH

By **Aryanna**

A KINGPIN'S AMBITON

A KINGPIN'S AMBITION **II**

I MURDER FOR THE DOUGH

By **Ambitious**

TRUE SAVAGE I II III IV V VI VII

DOPE BOY MAGIC I, II, III

MIDNIGHT CARTEL I II III

CITY OF KINGZ I II

NIGHTMARE ON SILENT AVE

THE PLUG OF LIL MEXICO II

CLASSIC CITY

By **Chris Green**

A DOPEBOY'S PRAYER

By **Eddie "Wolf" Lee**

THE KING CARTEL **I, II & III**

By **Frank Gresham**

THESE NIGGAS AIN'T LOYAL **I, II & III**

By **Nikki Tee**

GANGSTA SHYT **I II &III**

By **CATO**

THE ULTIMATE BETRAYAL

By **Phoenix**

BOSS'N UP **I , II & III**

By **Royal Nicole**

I LOVE YOU TO DEATH

By **Destiny J**

I RIDE FOR MY HITTA

I STILL RIDE FOR MY HITTA

By **Misty Holt**

LOVE & CHASIN' PAPER

By **Qay Crockett**

TO DIE IN VAIN

SINS OF A HUSTLA

By **ASAD**

BROOKLYN HUSTLAZ

By **Boogsy Morina**

BROOKLYN ON LOCK I & II

By **Sonovia**

GANGSTA CITY

By **Teddy Duke**

A DRUG KING AND HIS DIAMOND I & II III

A DOPEMAN'S RICHES

HER MAN, MINE'S TOO I, II

CASH MONEY HO'S

THE WIFEY I USED TO BE I II

PRETTY GIRLS DO NASTY THINGS

By **Nicole Goosby**

TRAPHOUSE KING **I II & III**

KINGPIN KILLAZ I II III

STREET KINGS I II

PAID IN BLOOD **I II**

CARTEL KILLAZ I II III

DOPE GODS I II

By **Hood Rich**

LIPSTICK KILLAH **I, II, III**

CRIME OF PASSION I II & III

FRIEND OR FOE I II III

By **Mimi**

STEADY MOBBN' **I, II, III**

THE STREETS STAINED MY SOUL I II III

By **Marcellus Allen**

WHO SHOT YA **I, II, III**

SON OF A DOPE FIEND I II

HEAVEN GOT A GHETTO I II

SKI MASK MONEY I II

Renta

GORILLAZ IN THE BAY **I II III IV**

TEARS OF A GANGSTA I II

3X KRAZY I II

STRAIGHT BEAST MODE I II

DE'KARI

TRIGGADALE I II III

MURDAROBER WAS THE CASE I II

Elijah R. Freeman

GOD BLESS THE TRAPPERS I, II, III

THESE SCANDALOUS STREETS I, II, III

FEAR MY GANGSTA I, II, III IV, V

THESE STREETS DON'T LOVE NOBODY I, II

BURY ME A G I, II, III, IV, V

A GANGSTA'S EMPIRE I, II, III, IV

THE DOPEMAN'S BODYGAURD I II

THE REALEST KILLAZ I II III

THE LAST OF THE OGS I II III

Tranay Adams

THE STREETS ARE CALLING

Duquie Wilson

MARRIED TO A BOSS I II III

By Destiny Skai & Chris Green

KINGZ OF THE GAME I II III IV V VI VII

CRIME BOSS

Playa Ray

SLAUGHTER GANG I II III

RUTHLESS HEART I II III

By Willie Slaughter

FUK SHYT

By Blakk Diamond

DON'T F#CK WITH MY HEART I II

By Linnea

ADDICTED TO THE DRAMA I II III

IN THE ARM OF HIS BOSS II

By Jamila

YAYO I II III IV

A SHOOTER'S AMBITION I II

BRED IN THE GAME

By S. Allen

TRAP GOD I II III

RICH $AVAGE I II III

MONEY IN THE GRAVE I II III

By Martell Troublesome Bolden

FOREVER GANGSTA I II

GLOCKS ON SATIN SHEETS I II

By Adrian Dulan

TOE TAGZ I II III IV

LEVELS TO THIS SHYT I II

IT'S JUST ME AND YOU

By Ah'Million

KINGPIN DREAMS I II III

RAN OFF ON DA PLUG

By Paper Boi Rari

CONFESSIONS OF A GANGSTA I II III IV

CONFESSIONS OF A JACKBOY I II

By Nicholas Lock

I'M NOTHING WITHOUT HIS LOVE

SINS OF A THUG

TO THE THUG I LOVED BEFORE

A GANGSTA SAVED XMAS

IN A HUSTLER I TRUST

By Monet Dragun

CAUGHT UP IN THE LIFE I II III

THE STREETS NEVER LET GO I II III

By Robert Baptiste

NEW TO THE GAME I II III

MONEY, MURDER & MEMORIES I II III

By **Malik D. Rice**

LIFE OF A SAVAGE I II III IV

A GANGSTA'S QUR'AN I II III IV

MURDA SEASON I II III

GANGLAND CARTEL I II III

CHI'RAQ GANGSTAS I II III IV

KILLERS ON ELM STREET I II III

JACK BOYZ N DA BRONX I II III

A DOPEBOY'S DREAM I II III

JACK BOYS VS DOPE BOYS I II III

COKE GIRLZ

COKE BOYS

SOSA GANG I II

BRONX SAVAGES

BODYMORE KINGPINS

BLOOD OF A GOON

By Romell Tukes

LOYALTY AIN'T PROMISED I II

By Keith Williams
QUIET MONEY I II III
THUG LIFE I II III
EXTENDED CLIP I II
A GANGSTA'S PARADISE
By Trai'Quan
THE STREETS MADE ME I II III
By Larry D. Wright
THE ULTIMATE SACRIFICE I, II, III, IV, V, VI
KHADIFI
IF YOU CROSS ME ONCE I II
ANGEL I II III IV
IN THE BLINK OF AN EYE
By Anthony Fields
THE LIFE OF A HOOD STAR
By Ca$h & Rashia Wilson
THE STREETS WILL NEVER CLOSE I II III
By K'ajji
CREAM I II III
THE STREETS WILL TALK
By Yolanda Moore
NIGHTMARES OF A HUSTLA I II III
By King Dream
CONCRETE KILLA I II III
VICIOUS LOYALTY I II III
By Kingpen
HARD AND RUTHLESS I II
MOB TOWN 251
THE BILLIONAIRE BENTLEYS I II III

REAL G'S MOVE IN SILENCE

By Von Diesel

GHOST MOB

Stilloan Robinson

MOB TIES I II III IV V VI

SOUL OF A HUSTLER, HEART OF A KILLER I II

GORILLAZ IN THE TRENCHES I II

By SayNoMore

BODYMORE MURDERLAND I II III

THE BIRTH OF A GANGSTER I II

By Delmont Player

FOR THE LOVE OF A BOSS

By C. D. Blue

MOBBED UP I II III IV

THE BRICK MAN I II III IV V

THE COCAINE PRINCESS I II III IV V VI VII VIII

By King Rio

KILLA KOUNTY I II III IV

By Khufu

MONEY GAME I II

By Smoove Dolla

A GANGSTA'S KARMA I II III

By FLAME

KING OF THE TRENCHES I II III

by **GHOST & TRANAY ADAMS**

QUEEN OF THE ZOO I II

By **Black Migo**

GRIMEY WAYS I II III

By Ray Vinci

XMAS WITH AN ATL SHOOTER

By Ca$h & Destiny Skai

KING KILLA

By Vincent "Vitto" Holloway

BETRAYAL OF A THUG I II

By Fre$h

THE MURDER QUEENS I II

By Michael Gallon

TREAL LOVE

By Le'Monica Jackson

FOR THE LOVE OF BLOOD I II

By Jamel Mitchell

HOOD CONSIGLIERE I II

By Keese

PROTÉGÉ OF A LEGEND I II III

LOVE IN THE TRENCHES

By Corey Robinson

BORN IN THE GRAVE I II III

By Self Made Tay

MOAN IN MY MOUTH

By XTASY

TORN BETWEEN A GANGSTER AND A GENTLEMAN

By J-BLUNT & Miss Kim

LOYALTY IS EVERYTHING I II

Molotti

HERE TODAY GONE TOMORROW

By Fly Rock

PILLOW PRINCESS

By S. Hawkins

NAÏVE TO THE STREETS
WOMEN LIE MEN LIE I II III
GIRLS FALL LIKE DOMINOS
STACK BEFORE YOU SPURLGE
By A. Roy Milligan

BOOKS BY LDP'S CEO, CA$H

TRUST IN NO MAN

TRUST IN NO MAN 2

TRUST IN NO MAN 3

BONDED BY BLOOD

SHORTY GOT A THUG

THUGS CRY

THUGS CRY 2

THUGS CRY 3

TRUST NO BITCH

TRUST NO BITCH 2

TRUST NO BITCH 3

TIL MY CASKET DROPS

RESTRAINING ORDER

RESTRAINING ORDER 2

IN LOVE WITH A CONVICT

LIFE OF A HOOD STAR

XMAS WITH AN ATL SHOOTER